THE WAY HOME

SHARON MANIACI

The Way Home
Written by Sharon Maniaci
Edited by Marla McKenna
Cover Design by Michael Nicloy
Interior Layout by Griff Mill

Cover Photo by Sheila Struckmeyer
Author Photo by Allyson Hoxsey

ISBN: 978-1-957351-39-1

PUBLISHED BY NICO 11 PUBLISHING & DESIGN
MUKWONAGO, WISCONSIN
www.nico11publishing.com

Be well read.

Quantity orders may be made by contacting the publisher:
mike@nico11publishing.com

Printed in the United States of America

THIS WORK CONTAINS MATURE AND SENSITIVE MATERIAL AND LANGUAGE WHICH MAY BE TRIGGERING TO THE READER.

TO THE READER

The first thing I want to say is, I thank you all from the bottom of my heart for being so patient as I completed this second book. I had already started on this one before *THE RIDE HOME* was published, in fact, I was about half way finished, or so I thought, when my friend Tom Frase came to me and said "Hey, can we talk about your first book?" After a lengthy discussion, Tom began to help me work through the creative process better than I had been before. As someone who studied Anthropology, I learned of course, about Evolution, but from Tom, I learned how to evolve from being just a Writer to becoming a Storyteller. I never realized there was a difference until that day we sat and talked about the first book.

I know a lot of you reached out after reading it, telling me how brave I am for telling that story, for making it known the horrendous things that happened that day, and for that, I thank you. The road to *THE WAY HOME* has been long and tedious, but well worth the journey in so many ways. Thank you all as you take this journey with me, for your love and support. I would truly have no reason to keep writing if it weren't for those of you who have asked me, "Is there more?" I will keep telling the stories for as long as you, the reader, ask for more.

All My Love and Thanks –
Sharon Maniaci

FOREWORD

I heard from a professional writer that 98% of all writers say they're writing, but they're not finishing and the 2% who do, well, they're so emotionally tied to their story that they are incapable of receiving feedback.

Writing is not easy. Too many distractions and excuses not to write. Being an aspiring writer myself, I know the pitfalls.

Dealing with trauma is also not easy. Our society doesn't hold in high regard those who are dealing with past trauma. Hide in the dark, speak behind closed doors… whisper.

After reading Sharon's first book, The Ride Home, and talking with her, I learned of her trauma, and I am amazed how she found a way to cope and live her life.

Sharon and I graduated from high school together, long ago, in a galaxy far, far away. Recently, we connected as we have a need, a strong need, to tell stories. Our sense of humor is similar… dark and twisted and in the gutter for the most part. This helps with writing and creates a space to push boundaries and explore unforeseen trajectories.

I applaud Sharon as she gets shit done. She doesn't talk about being a writer, she writes. She takes feedback and digests it, hoping to make her writing and storytelling better. (P.S. Writing and storytelling are two different things.)

Sharon has found a way to stand up to her trauma, face it mano-a-mano and laugh. Through writing she is exploring her past, present and future and has discovered and is discovering herself. She can laugh at the unlaughable and weep at the unlaughable… her choice.

Quentin Tarantino found a way to tell stories about the way they might have happened in Inglourious Basterds and Once Upon a Time in Hollywood. Much the same in *The Way Home*. A sequel to The Ride Home. This book fills in details from the first story and explores many of the ways people become monsters and how people can overcome tragedy.

Again, I applaud Sharon for giving herself to you, the reader, and to her friends and family.

To Sharon and the Wentzville Class of 1988… one bad-ass-class!

Thomas Frase

THE
WAY HOME

CHAPTER 1

AUGUST 2014

When Kris woke up, she was lying on the couch, and Tony was sitting next to her. Ronnie was sitting on the love seat near her. When she first looked at Ronnie, she took a moment to let it all sink in and that Ronnie was there. That is when Kris started sobbing. She knew in that instant why Ronnie had shown up to the house.

"I did not do this Ronnie. I swear it on my own life. I did not kill Mack."

Tony was holding her tightly against his chest. She could hear and feel his heartbeat. It started to soothe her. Ronnie reached over and put her hand on Kris's leg. She suddenly felt very calm, as though she melted into a cloud.

"I know you did not do this, Kris. Terry and I both know you didn't."

She pulled a piece of paper out of her briefcase. "I managed to pull some strings, and we're going to do an arraignment over video conference. Surprisingly, they let me come because we have a history. We are going to coordinate with local law enforcement and will all go to the court building from there."

"Do you need me to get a number for the police department?" Kris asked.

"No, I have the name and number for a detective. Let me give him a call and let him know we are coming down to the station. I will need you to tell me how to get there," Ronnie told her.

"Oh, I will tell you how to get there alright," Kris said as she smirked.

"Still a smart ass I see. That is a good thing."

Ronnie made her call and within ten minutes, they all three left the house. The 15-minute drive felt like it took forever. They were directed to meet with one of the circuit court judges in chambers for the video conference. Kris's attorney, Penelope, was also on the call.

The Circuit Court judge for the City of St. Louis began reading the charges against Kris. "Mrs. Parker, you have been indicted on the following charges: Murder in the Second Degree; Assault in the First Degree; Sodomy in the Second Degree and Tampering with Evidence. How do you plead?"

Kris was reeling from all the charges listed, almost passing out. *How in the world can anyone think I am capable of these things*? Kris wondered. "Not Guilty Your Honor."

"Does the state have recommendations on bail?"

"We do. We are asking that the defendant be remanded to the local jail in Virginia until trial Your Honor."

Penelope spoke up. "Your Honor, Mrs. Parker is not a flight risk. She is a former police officer with the City of St. Louis and is currently employed at a university and an active volunteer for two local animal shelters as a foster. She is married to a retired Chief Petty Officer of the United States Navy, who is frequently on business trips with his current job with the United States Government. This makes her the sole caretaker of the house and their pets. Once again, she has no reason to flee. I am going to request that Mrs. Parker be released on house arrest. She can conduct her work for the university at home and the animal shelter she volunteers for is only a short distance from her residence."

The judge looked in Kris's direction and asked, "Mrs. Parker, do you have a current passport?"

"Yes sir, I do. I have never used it, but it will not expire until 2020."

"So, you have never been out of the country Mrs. Parker?"

"Yes, your honor, I have. When my husband and I lived in San Diego, we would go to Mexico occasionally, but only to Tijuana, and passports were not required then."

"In normal circumstances I would remand you, but I am not going to do that in this case. Given your current ties to the community, the fact that you haven't had as much as a speeding ticket and your former employment as an officer, I am going to place you on house arrest, but only AFTER 10 percent of a million-dollar bond is secured."

The Circuit Attorney, Richard McCullen's face turned a deep shade of purple at the judge's announcement and began to argue why Kris should not be allowed to be released. "Your Honor! This is extremely unprecedented! This woman is accused of numerous violent acts that have resulted in the death of a well-respected former officer of the police department. Had he been an active-duty officer, she would be looking at the death penalty!"

"Counselor, I am fully aware of the law. If I wasn't, I would not be sitting in this chair. As it is, I AM sitting in this chair, and it is MY decision to make."

Richard's face turned more purple than Kris ever thought a human's face could.

"Mrs. Parker, until you have made bond, you will be held in the local jail in Virginia. Detective Lowell, would it be safe to say that you have been removed from the investigation of this case?"

"Yes, Your Honor. The department has removed me from the case. In addition, I volunteered to take a leave of absence until I am told I can come back." What Ronnie did not tell the judge is that while she was not able to investigate in an official capacity, she had every intention of doing some investigation on her own. She knew her friend did not murder Mack, and she was definitely going to find out who did. On a personal level, Ronnie was fine with the fact that Mack was dead, especially knowing what he did to her friend.

While Kris had every reason to hurt Mack just as he hurt her, Ronnie understood her friend well enough to know that the level of violence inflicted on Mack was not something Kris was capable of. Ronnie was more than aware of what was done to Mack, and even if Kris had the mental capacity to do those things and not feel any remorse, there was no way Kris could have physically done them ... at least not alone.

Ronnie knew that whoever did kill Mack, needed the strength to take him to his knees to subdue him. Mack was found tied, spread eagle, to stakes that had been hammered into a concrete slab. She knew Kris, but she also knew Mack, and she knew he was not the kind of person to go down without a fight. A person Kris's size could not physically do something like that alone. The worst part about the entire situation was that nobody other than she or Terry were thinking along those lines. The police department and the courts were so eager to condemn the first person on the list of the most probable suspects, that the bigger picture was being ignored and the tunnel vision was narrowing in on Kris.

CHAPTER 2

Throughout his college years, Mack continued to prey on vulnerable women. He always made sure there was another guy with him, someone he could share activities with … someone he could look at to get and maintain his erection.

He had been in the police department for a few years before he learned about "Roofies," the scientific name for Rohypnol. He was married, settled into a home, and worked opposite shift from his wife so he did not have to have too much interaction with her. She worked at a bank, so she was gone during the day while he was either sleeping in or at CODE 40. The two owners of CODE 40 were two retired police officers, and they were open very early in the morning until 3 a.m. They made sure it was a "cop" bar, a place where the officer who worked the overnight shift had a place to unwind as well.

They served bar food and of course drinks, but for Mack, one of the owners and sometimes bartender, served up "Roofies" when Mack requested it. There were plenty of "Badge Bunnies," the term for women who would flirt with cops in the hopes of marrying one of them.

Many of the ladies flirted with Mack, but they would leave after he bought them drinks all night.

Some of them had the audacity to turn Mack down after finding out he was married. A couple of them were bold enough to tell him they thought he was gay, and he really didn't like it when they said that. They weren't wrong, but it was something Mack continued to deny. He didn't accept it just as it wasn't accepted in this job any more than it was in football.

He believed that being gay made him less of a man, but when he was with a woman from the bar, he usually talked another guy into participating in the sex. Most didn't turn the offer down, because for some men, it was their fantasy to take turns with a woman. Mack banked on this idea because it was the only way he could be with men which was his true intention. When he started to train Shaen, he had a new "partner in crime."

At first, Shaen wasn't on board with Mack's antics because he was engaged and too new on the department, meaning he could be fired for any reason, including anything Mack made up.

After the first couple of times, Shaen became more comfortable with his participation. Mack could count on Shaen's discretion, because he knew Shaen was worried about keeping his job.

What Mack didn't know was that Shaen was gathering just as much ammunition against Mack as what Mack was against Shaen. It was only a matter of time before one of them figured out how to use it against the other.

CHAPTER 3

Mack's phone chirped and he looked at the number. *It's about time he did what he was told.* Mack thought. "Did you get in touch with her?" he asked Shaen.

"Yes. I am meeting with her tomorrow. When I am through talking to her, I will call you and we will set up a place to meet. I am really getting tired of these phone calls."

"I will be waiting for your phone call, Shaen. Do not fuck this up," Mack told him.

"Fuck you, Mack." With that, Shaen hung up the phone, grabbed his keys, and went to the store.

1996

Mack only briefly saw Kris at work when he was going off shift and she was coming on. He worked overnights and she was on rotating days and afternoons. She was younger and he knew she was single. Life was not that great at the Parkins household. Mack's wife worked during the day, and they did not get to see much of each other since they had opposite shifts. His wife told him the only thing she liked about him working the overnight shift was the extra money on his paycheck. The stress and strain the work put on their marriage found Mack in a sexless marriage, so he found his release elsewhere.

He kept thinking back to the last woman he picked up in a cop bar. *She had been teasing him all evening. Mack was usually at the bar in the mornings due to his shift, but he was off for a few days and his wife was out of town visiting family. He was enjoying the alone time, sitting at the bar, and talking to some of the people from work. The woman approached him, striking up a conversation. She was not drop dead gorgeous, but he couldn't take his eyes off her either. She was beautiful in a plain way, and he could tell she knew it. She had been toying with Mack since she walked up to him—running her hand very lightly across the small of his back, leaning in like she was listening to his stories, her breasts brushing against his arm. He would not dare stand up at this point but sitting there was just as uncomfortable.*

During the conversation, she told him she had to run outside to answer a phone call. When she stepped away from the bar, he bought her a drink and as she walked back in, the bartender slid the drinks across the bar. The bartender tapped the edge of one of the glasses when Mack caught his eye. Mack slid that very same glass to the spot in front of the woman. When she sat down, Mack asked, "Is everything okay?"

"Oh, yes. It was a work thing. I had to make sure my meeting tomorrow is set up properly."

"Oh, good. What time is your meeting?" he asked her.

"Not until eleven. It is a lunch meeting. Why so curious?" she asked, running a finger over Mack's hand.

"I thought maybe we could finish our drinks and go back to my house."

"Aren't you married?" she asked.

"Yes, but she is out of town for the next week."

"I don't know. It seems a little risky to me. I don't really know you."

"Well, you are in a cop bar, surrounded by police officers. The bartender/owner is a former police officer. You couldn't be in better hands. My entire family comes from a lengthy line of police officers," Mack reassured her.

The woman thought about it for a minute and told Mack, "Mack, it is Mack, right?"

"Yes."

"Mack, I just can't tonight. I cannot miss my meeting in the morning, and I have things to take care of before it starts. I need to be up early, and I should not have had this last drink."

"Well, now that it is in front of you, you have to finish it. I was paying attention to what the bartender was making and bought it for you. At least finish it and we can keep chatting. You can tell me about your work, what you like to do in your off time … that kind of thing."

"Fair enough," she replied. "I will finish this, but it has to be the last one."

"I understand. This is my last one too."

A couple of weeks later, after having surgery, Mack was put on desk duty until he could return to full duty. He was seeing more of Kris because she rotated to the afternoon shift, and he was on the same shift at this point. They began talking when she was coming out of roll call, and he would give her the handheld radio. They would talk any time they were working together, and after about three weeks, he told her that a bunch of people were grabbing food and drinks after shift, asking her if she wanted to meet them. "Sure," Kris told him. "I don't have plans tonight."

"Great. We are meeting at CODE 40. Do you know where that is?"

"Yes, of course, see you there."

From that night on, Kris would meet Mack and others at CODE 40 for drinks whenever she was able. A couple of months later, they all rotated to the day shift, so the meetups usually happened on days off. They met one evening after work and Kris came into the bar, visibly upset. "What's wrong?" Mack asked her. She launched into some troubles she was having with a couple of her co-workers on the squad that were in her academy class. To top it off, the Sgt. of the squad had been all over Kris for stupid things. While everyone else was roaming the district, Sgt. wanted Kris to remain strictly within the boundaries of her patrol area.

"I swear Mack, there is not one thing I can do right in this woman's eyes right now. I just want to be away from her."

"You know what the problem is don't you Kris?"

"If I knew, I would fix it."

"You have been given a bad rap from the start Kris. Your training officer screwed you by telling people you couldn't be trusted. Second, you work for a sergeant who was among the first of the female officers to be hired to the department, so she has to keep proving that she can do the job as well as any man that came before her. Lastly, you are good at what you do, and she is threatened by that."

"Well, what do I do then? How do I fix this?" she asked.

"Truthfully … I think you need to go to the overnight shift. There are very few commanders on at that time, you can be proactive and reactive to calls; the nights go by faster and the night crew really does stick together."

"I don't know. I am not much of a night person."

"You get used to it; I promise. Go talk to the lieutenant today and see what he says. I bet you can be on the night shift by next week. There is a new academy class coming out, so they will have someone to fill the spot eventually."

"You know, I think I will. I need to get away from these people, and the pay will be better too."

They finished their drinks and food, and he walked her to her car. They stood there talking outside her car and when she unlocked and opened her car door, he leaned in and kissed her. Thank god she is parked in a secluded area he thought to himself. She was kissing him back, and it all led to much more. Mack leaned her back on the hood of her car, kissing her, exploring her body with his hands, and then they moved to the back seat of her car. Despite being in the back seat, the sex was amazing. When they finished, she laughed and said, "I haven't done this in a car since I was in college and living at home."

"Maybe next time, we can be indoors. What if someone calls the cops on us?" he asked as they both began laughing.

The sex continued for months. Mack ended up with a probationary officer in his car because

that guy's training officer was on leave. Kris started to become a little more distant, and Mack

was sure she was seeing another police officer. He didn't really like it, but there wasn't much he

could do about it since he was married and had no right to be exclusive. He and the probation

officer, Shaen Finney, would go out, but Shaen wouldn't stay out long because he had a fiancé

at home. Mack was finding himself in need of physical company more and more. He would go to CODE 40 on his own, pick-up women and buy them drinks, despite them telling him they

weren't interested in more than just talking. It was always the same excuse too. "If you weren't

married ..." This included some of the female officers too. Always playing and teasing but never

following through. *I will still have them,* he thought. *All I have to do is buy them that one last*

drink.

When Shaen graduated from college, he applied for the St. Louis Metropolitan Police

Academy, pausing his blackmailing activities to concentrate on getting through. *'I have to make*

it through because once I have that badge'... Shaen ended up developing an obsession for a

civilian instructor. She taught First Aid and CPR. He figured he would wait to see how he could

get her to bed. Now he had to be careful because he was also engaged. He loved his fiancé as

much as he was capable of loving someone. He thought his mom loved him, and if she did, it

wasn't enough for her to stop what her own brother did to him.

Shaen was accepted to the academy and graduated in mid-summer. He was assigned to the

9th District as a Probationary Police Officer. Like every officer before him, he would undergo Field

Training for six months. After that he would be on his own if he passed. A few weeks into his

training, his FTO, or "Field Training Officer," went on vacation with his family, so Shaen was

provided with a temporary FTO, Mack Parkins. They worked the night shift, which started at

11 p.m. The bars and nightclubs in the area, including around two elite universities, did not close until 3 a.m. This also gave both Mack and Shaen some target rich hunting grounds.

Mack would frequently hang out with a female officer in the 5th District, which bordered the 9th

on some streets. The first night they rode together, Shaen was driving, while Mack talked on the

phone to someone named "Kris." Shaen couldn't hear Kris's voice, so when Mack was hanging

up the call and told Kris he couldn't wait to be with her again, Shaen glanced at Mack, thinking,

'I wish I would have known they were going to put me with some fag'.

Now it was Mack's turn to catch someone watching HIM. "What are you looking at Probe?"

"Nothing. Sorry," he replied.

Mack just looked at him. "Just drive to the Del Taco so I can meet up with Kris really quick."

Shaen did as he was told, and they backed into a parking spot, making sure to park in two

spots so Kris had a place to park as well. Kris backed up to the passenger side of the car, so she

was on Mack's side of the car. When her window rolled down, Shaen saw her lean down a little

to say "Hi." When he saw her face and heard her voice, realizing "Kris" was a female, he sighed

and what he thought was barely audible "Oh, thank God it's a woman."

Mack looked at him and said, "What did you just say?"

"Nothing. I didn't say a thing."

"Shaen, this is Kris, short for KRISTINE, Clarke."

"Hey Kris. I have seen you around the station, just haven't had a chance to talk." Just before

he greeted her, he took off his mirrored sunglasses, but kept the black leather, half-fingered

driving gloves on.

Kris did her best not to smile and laugh. He was the joke of the station because of the glasses

and gloves. "Hey Shaen. Nice to formally meet you."

Mack spoke up, "I was telling Shaen about CODE 40. He has wedding planning events the

next couple of weeks, but we should all meet there one morning."

"Sounds good to me Mack," Kris told him.

Shaen had his leverage …

Kris did finally go on the night shift, and she thanked Mack for the suggestion. She was loving it, and Mack was happy for her. He was also a little frustrated with her because their encounters were dwindling. Now the only time they would get together was when they had a day off at the same time. On occasion she would meet him on her night off while he was working. One evening she met him, and they found an alley in his patrol area to park and had sex in his patrol car. One of the other cars drove past them, and it apparently got back to her partner. Andrew, Kris's partner, approached him one night and told Mack to keep it in his pants where Kris was concerned. "Andrew, you can mind your own fucking business. She is an adult and can fuck who she wants."

"Mack, I have heard stories about what you have been doing, and I am telling you right now, if she gets hurt, your daddy's rank won't help you out of trouble."

"Fuck off Andrew, and just do your job," Mack said, walking away in a huff.

CHAPTER 4

The following week, Mack was on shift in his district and Kris and Andrew were patrolling in theirs. They were riding in an unmarked car, Kris driving, when a call came out for an "Officer in Need of Aid." On the way to the call, Kris missed a blinking red light, the driver of another vehicle did not yield to their emergency lights, and Kris and Andrew were T-boned. Everyone was okay, just shaken up, but Kris was more shaken than she realized and was a bundle of nerves. That morning after work, Mack approached her as they were leaving the station. "You up for a drink? A few of us are going to CODE 40 for a while."

As he asked, and Kris responded, Andrew was walking by, glaring at Mack. "Sure. I think I could use it today. I don't want to stay too long though because we work again tonight. That incident drained me for some reason."

"That's fine. I completely understand."

Once they were at the bar, Kris ordered her drink, Mack paying close attention to what she was having. She ordered some food, which was soaking up any alcohol she was having. She ordered a second, told the bartender she needed her check and nursed the second drink. "Hey," Kris said to Mack, "Could you watch my stuff, I have to use the restroom."

"Sure, but you know, once you break the seal ..." and they laughed. While she was gone, he told Shaen, "We are going to have some fun today dude."

"What are you going to do?"

"WE are going to fuck the shit out of her. You know she wants you right."

"Mack, I am engaged. I'm not about to cheat on my fiancé."

"Think of it as an early bachelor party. It will be fun, I promise." Mack took Kris's keys off the bar and put them in his pocket.

Shaen shook his head and said, "You know what, you are right. The fiancé has been withholding lately, and I could use some fun."

Mack ordered a second drink, the bartender tapped the edge of the glass and put it in front of Kris's seat at the bar. When she came back, Mack told her he ordered another drink because the one she had was too watered down. She told him she wanted to go home, that she was tired.

"Just finish this, and I will give you a ride home," Mack told her.

CHAPTER 5

Kris was escorted to the jail after the hearing. As she and the sheriff's deputy made their way to prisoner processing, Tony, Penelope and now Ronnie were all making calls to get Kris out of jail as soon as humanly possible. Ronnie felt terrible because she was the only one who could not contribute financially to the bail money. She could not be tied to any portion of Kris's case at this point. Ronnie would have to testify about the initial portion of the investigation, as would Terry, since they initially interviewed her. Ronnie would also have to testify at the hearing and place Kris under arrest. The good news about the later situations, is that there was another person there witnessing her actions and would be able to confirm everything Ronnie did was by the book.

The sheriff took Kris down to the booking area, but before they left, Tony, Ronnie and Penelope were already making phone calls. "Baby, I promise you, you won't be in there long. We will all still be here after your bond is posted to take you home," Tony said. Now, as she was walking with the deputy, thankfully without handcuffs, Kris began sweating and began to cry. Ronnie had pleaded with the deputy to leave the cuffs off of Kris because she knew it would send Kris into a panic. Kris walked with her hands in front of her, with the deputy barely holding onto Kris's arm.

"Thank you for being so kind," Kris told the young man walking her down the hall. She truly was grateful because she knew that other cops would wonder why he was being so nice to a "cop killer."

"It's not a problem ma'am. Your friend said you were a police officer with told me what happened, and she doesn't seem to be the sort of person who would lie, especially about something like that."

"No, she wouldn't. She is a good cop and an amazing friend. I would trust her with my life."

"It appears you already are," the deputy said to her.

"Yes, I guess you are right. I'm putting my faith, trust, and life in her hands and have been since this whole thing started."

"Yes ma'am. I can see that."

They walked in silence the last 50 feet to the processing room. When they walked in, the deputy looked at the woman working behind the desk and said, "Did you get the cell ready?"

"Yes, everything is just as you asked."
"Thank you," the deputy turned to Kris and explained to her, "I am going to get your prints really quick and then take pictures. Instead of putting you with a bunch of people in a holding cell, I am going to put you in a regular cell with someone. She is waiting for her turn in court, so she is alone."

"Okay," Kris said. She was listening to the deputy talk but was not processing what he said. All she heard was a drowned-out voice in what seemed like slow motion. It felt like she was in a movie, where the person was waking up after being struck in the head. Everything was fuzzy and she was getting hot again. Suddenly she heard exactly what the deputy was saying,

"Are you back with me Mrs. Parker?"

"Yes, I'm sorry. I have never experienced this from this side of the fence."

"I understand. Let's get you started, so we can get you out of here as soon as possible."

The first thing they did was a quick pat down, even though she had made it into the court building without any detectors going off. As Kris was patted down by the female deputy who came in the room, an overwhelming erotic feeling overcame her. '*What's this? Go away, not now*', she thought. Flashes of different, intense feelings were coming and going without rhyme or reason. Then she focused and imagined she was back in the academy when they were practicing the pat downs and hand cuffing. It wasn't until they put her behind the camera that the entire process began to sink in and the other intense feelings quickly vanished. She started sweating again and could feel her face flush with red. '*What the hell is happening? This isn't real*'. She thought. Kris felt like she had been there hours, but in reality it was only a few minutes.

CHAPTER 6

When her photos had been taken, the deputy led Kris to a small machine that looked like a printer or scanner for an office. "We do digital fingerprinting now. It's just like the 10-print card, and it will show you where to put your fingers, just less messy." Kris suddenly started to cry and shake uncontrollably. Within three minutes of this process, she couldn't breathe and experienced physical pain with every breath she tried to take.

She was having a panic and asthma attack at the same time. The male deputy told the female to get Kris in a chair, and he ran out of the room. He came back a short time later with a paramedic in tow. The paramedic placed a mask over Kris's nose and mouth and told her to take slow, deep breaths.

Kris was still crying, but her breathing was more regular. "Are you okay, ma'am?" the paramedic asked her after a few minutes.

Kris shook her head "yes."

"Are you ready for me to take the mask away?"

Again, she shook her head in the affirmative. When he took the mask away, she reached up, wiped her eyes with the back of her hand, looked at the deputies and said, "Okay, I am ready."

"Don't worry, the woman you will be with is harmless. She is one of our frequent fliers here," the female deputy told her. She put her hand in the middle of Kris's back and led her down a short hallway. She opened the cell door and told the lady sitting on the top bunk, "Dee Dee, this is Kris, and she won't be here long, so be nice."

"You got it boss," the woman replied.

The woman was older than Kris expected. "Go ahead and sit on that bottom bunk, hunnie. I won't bite. My name is Dee Dee, but you heard that."

"Yes ma'am," Kris replied.

"I would say it is nice to meet you, but it probably isn't so nice for you, is it?"

"No, no offense."

"None taken, sugar. It's never nice sitting in here, but I am sure they told you I am a frequent flier here. That means I am here regularly. They like to bring all the newbies to me because I ain't nasty to nobody. Not like those so-called women in the holding cell. Some of them are mean as snakes. What you here for?"

"I just had an arraignment with the courts in St. Louis. I am being charged with murder and a few other things," Kris replied.

"Girl, you don't look like a killer. Who did ya bump off?"

"I didn't kill anyone, but I am accused of killing a former co-worker from the St. Louis Police Department."

"DAMN!!! You went and killed a cop? Good for you, hunnie!" Dee Dee exclaimed.

"I did not kill him or anyone else. I haven't even seen the man in nearly 20 years," Kris insisted.

"Well, let's just say you DID do it, why are you being accused of it?"

"When I was a police officer, the dead cop and another cop drugged me and raped me."

"Shit girl, I would own that shit even if I hadn't done it. Let me guess, not a damn thing happened to them for raping you, did it?"

"No," Kris said through tears of disbelief and fear.

"And this shitty ass man turns up dead, and because they didn't get in trouble for what they did to you, you are automatically the killer. I hate to say it, but that it does not surprise me one bit, hunnie. It's a man's world, and we will always take the blame."

Kris started crying even harder now, and she was shaking. It was extremely cold in the cell, and there was nothing but a thin blanket to cover up with. "Do they always keep it so cold in here?" she asked.

"Oh yeah, sugar. It's so germs don't spread. There are some nasty women up in here. I'm not someone to worry about though. You won't catch anything from me. Then again, if you aren't here long, you won't have time to catch anything from anyone. If you were going to be here longer, I may be tempted to make you my girlfriend. You sure are cute."

This was overheard by the female deputy, who yelled from her spot at the end of the hall.

"Dee Dee, I said be nice. Quit scaring people."

"I'm just having some fun, boss. I wasn't serious. Did they set a bond for you?"

"Yes," she said through more tears.

"You must know some people if you got a bond, but let me tell you this, if you do find yourself behind bars longer or again, make sure you let people know you killed a cop."

"But I didn't …"

Dee Dee cut her off, "I know you said you didn't, but to save your ass in jail, you DID do it, catch what I am saying?"

Kris just stared blankly at her, still in complete shock over the entire situation. She was surprised she was able to hold the conversations up to this point. Dee Dee came down from her spot on the top bunk and sat next to Kris. When she sat down, Kris jumped. "I'm sorry girl, I didn't mean to scare you. It probably had something to do about that girlfriend comment I made, huh?"

Kris hesitates for a moment. "It didn't help."

"It is perfectly natural to be scared, especially after being a cop and sitting behind bars instead of putting someone else here."

"This is all a nightmare, isn't it? I'm not really here. Someone is going to wake me up and tell me this is all a sick joke," Kris said.

"No. This is all very real. All you can do now is pray this is the last time you see this side of the cell. You want company or for me to leave you be?"

"I need some space right now, please," Kris said as her eyes swelled with tears. Dee Dee backed away and the room grew dark. Dark and now hot. Hot flashes swirled in Kris as she covered her face with her hands.

Several hours later, the 10 percent bail had been sent to the court. Kris was fitted with an ankle monitor, and she was back home with Tony and the pets. When the three of them arrived back to the house,

Tony told Kris and Ronnie he was going to the store to get food for the grill. After he left, Kris Looked at Ronnie and said, "Ronnie, tell me honestly … how fucked am I?"

"Not as much as you would think given the current circumstances," as she pointed to Kris's ankle.

"Well, the current circumstances are indicating I am going to be spending the rest of my life behind bars."

"K.C., I am not going to let that happen. Surely you know that. I have already started looking into this and staying connected with Penelope to let her know what I have found so far. She has her own investigator, and I am unofficially helping them. Any leads I get, I let Terry and Penelope's investigator take."

"I thought Terry wasn't allowed to investigate because of our connection."

"The powers that be told him since he hasn't been in contact with you in any unofficial capacity, they will let him follow up on any leads that come in but not to go out and actively investigate. A new team is investigating your case."

"Oh, I just bet they are. They have me ready for prison already. They think I killed one of 'them' and there will not be any serious investigating going on. You know that Ronnie. You have been on the department long enough to know the wheels of justice are going to turn very slowly for me, if they turn at all."

"I will find my way around it all Kris, trust that I am telling you the truth. I would do anything for you, well, I wouldn't go to jail for you. I hear that place sucks," she said with a giggle.

Kris flipped Ronnie the middle finger, laughed and said, "Who would have thought the person who picked on me so horribly in the academy would be the person working twice as hard to save my ass?"

Ronnie grabbed Kris's face with both hands and looked her square in the eyes. "Kristine Clarke-Parker, surely you know by now that we are family and MOST of us, not including the shit heads that did this to you, are always here to protect and support each other. You know that not all police officers cover for each other the way this handful is.

We do not need a large contingency to fight this and make it right. We just need the RIGHT people to fight."

"Ronnie, thank you. You truly are an amazing friend, and I love you for that."

"Girl, I love you too. This is all going to be okay. I promise. You want to talk about where we are so far? Penelope told me I could fill you in up to this point."

"YES! Of course, I do."

CHAPTER 7

Ronnie and Kris talked about what had been found so far in the investigation, but only the information from Penelope's investigator.

Ronnie felt bad about keeping information from Kris, but she did not want her to get too hopeful. Ronnie had been following a path in the investigation with Penelope and her team that would change the game in a big way. She knew from the start Kris had not killed Mack and Ronnie would not stop until everyone else knew it too.

Tony arrived home with steak for the grill, and while he cooked outside and played with the pups, Kris made side dishes and talked with Ronnie. Ronnie was headed back to St. Louis the next day, so after dinner, the three of them sat and watched a movie. Despite it being August, it was cool enough after the sun went down to build a small fire in the fire pit after dinner. Kris was very much at peace outside by the lake. There were times she would sit there during the day before the sun got too hot, watching the gray herons hunt the bullfrogs. At night, the bullfrogs would start croaking, singing their own chorus. In the early spring, it was the spring peepers that comforted her. They reminded her of home, and she would give anything to be back there right now, but not under the circumstances she was currently in.

They decided to make s'mores and stayed up later than they should have. Everyone, especially Kris, was exhausted, but even that did not stop the laughter from the stories Ronnie and Kris were telling about their academy days, Kris's brief time on the streets working with Andrew, Wanda, and Ronnie. There were times she still really missed the job. It was a job she was good at and genuinely loved. Now, it felt as though that same place had betrayed her. She knew she was in the biggest fight of her life, and Ronnie was pivotal in saving her.

The next day, Ronnie, Kris, and Tony said their good-byes. Ronnie hugged Kris and reassured her, "This is all going to be okay Kris. I promise you that. When that monitor comes off, it is because you are walking from the courthouse a free woman."

"You cannot make those promises. It's not that I don't trust you or believe in you, but I don't want to get my hopes up. I know as well as you do what these assholes are capable of."

Ronnie looked at her dead in the eyes, "Some birds are meant to be caged and hope, hope is a good thing, and no good thing ever dies."

Kris stared back at her. "Shawshank, really?" They both laughed.

They hugged again, and Ronnie got on the road. Kris made Ronnie promise to check in periodically to make sure she wasn't too tired and made it home safely.

Mack sat in the small gym with the other boys in his health class. Today, the sixth graders had all been separated from each other for the day. The girls all went with the female gym teacher and the boys went with the male gym teacher in separate, smaller gyms. This was the age the schools in Texas thought it was necessary for students to learn about sexual reproduction and after they covered the basics in class, they would go into a little more detail, but it was necessary for the boys and girls to be in an environment where they could ask anything they wanted about sex and puberty.

The boys were all quiet while they waited for the gym teacher to show up. Even at 12 years old, Mack picked up on the bravado the boys were all displaying, talking about the girls in their class and how they noticed their boobs getting bigger, acting as if they had already had the opportunity to touch them. One of the boys started talking about a dream he had of one of the prettiest girls in the class and he woke up with his pants "wet." "Dude…" one of the other boys said, "That happened to me too!"

"Ya'll are peeing the bed and can't admit that you still need to be in diapers!" another boy said.

"Shut up man. It was not pee."

"Yeah, right … bed wetter."

"Take it back!" the first boy screamed.

"Bed wetter, bed wetter!!"

The first boy jumped at the bully and a fight broke out just as the teacher was walking in.

Mack jumped in to break it up. The entire time he was trying to break up the fight, he thought … this does not happen to me … heck, I don't even have dreams about girls. As he was breaking up the fight with a couple of other boys, he also thought about the male gym teacher. The gym teacher was new to the school, had only been out of college a year, and was a college athlete.

Mack thought about how well built the teacher was, admiring him and his physique. Suddenly, Mack could feel himself getting aroused, but he was not the only one who noticed. He had a grip on the bully while this was all happening. The bully felt Mack's sudden arousal and turned his meanness on Mack.

"WHAT THE HELL DUDE?! Is your pecker hard? Oh God, it is!" he yelled.

The rest of the boys joined in teasing Mack about being aroused while touching the other boys.

Mack tried to argue his way out of it, denying that touching the other boy had anything to do

with his physical reaction. "That is not what happened at all!" he said. "It started before that, when you were talking about Grace and her boobs."

"Whatever man, nobody believes you. I bet you pee your pants at night too. You better not have dreams about any of US!"

"Trust me, I wouldn't have dreams about your ugly ass face!" Mack said, knowing full well he dreamt about the teacher, and would, in fact, wake up the same way as the other boys who dreamt of Grace.

When Mack called the boy "ugly," that incited the kid even more and he lunged at Mack. A new fight ensued, but nobody dared jump in for fear of "exciting" Mack. About this time, the gym teacher and health teacher came running into the gym, pulling the two apart as he made a

threat of suspension if they did not stop. "What is going on boys?" he asked.

The boy who went after the bully spoke up. "Me and Jake were fighting because he kept calling me and a few of the other guys 'bed wetter,' and when Mack came to break it up, his pecker got hard, so then Mack called him 'ugly' and then THEY started fighting."

The teachers looked at each other, knowing this was not going to be an easy conversation.

"Everyone just sit down so we can get this going," the gym teacher said. The health teacher spoke up next.

"So, as you all know, we have been going over sexual reproduction in class. We separated you from the ladies so you can all feel free to ask us anything or have us explain anything to you that you may not feel comfortable saying in class or asking your parents. We are here to answer those questions or concerns."

Jake, the bully, was the first one to blurt something out. "Can you explain why these morons are wetting their beds at night?"

"Who is wetting the bed?"

"All of them apparently," Jake said. "They said they have dreams about one of the girls in class and wake up with their shorts wet."

'Dear God, this is going to be a long day'. The gym teacher thought.

The health teacher explained to the boys what was happening with their bodies, and there was nothing wrong with any of them. Jake puffed his chest out, "Well, it doesn't happen to me!" he said with a sense of pride.

"Maybe you are broke," one kid said.

'Maybe you don't like girls'. Mack thought.

At the same time, one of the other boys said out loud, "Probably because you are a fag, and you dream about boys, like Mack does!"

There was a burst of laughter and then one boy said, "Maybe they are dreaming of each other! Mack did get hard when he grabbed Jake!"

"Take it back you asshole!" Jake yelled.

At the same time, Mack and Jake went after the kid, which ended up with both in the principal's office, and a three-day suspension. As Mack was walking home, he was thinking of the day's events, about having to explain this to his parents as to why he was being suspended.

He knew at that moment everything the boys were saying was true. Mack did NOT like girls the same way the other boys did.

Even at the age of 11, Mack began to realize more and more, he felt different, but today just solidified it. Now he knew why he reacted to the gym teacher in the dreams and sometimes he would see him in the locker room. He also knew he would never be able to really be honest about how he feels or what he experiences; not with his family, friends, or church ... not any time soon, and DEFINITELY not while he lived in Texas.

He continued his walk home, trying to plan what he was going to say to his parents. His head was down, and he could see something weird on the sidewalk. As he approached, he realized it was a caterpillar. He knelt in front of it, watching it. He was watching because it was in the process of spinning a cocoon. Mack studied the caterpillar as it spun itself into the beautiful silk, in an almost effortless fashion. Mack was mesmerized as the caterpillar worked to become something beautiful and free—something he would never become.

He slowly stood, knowing he would have to eventually go home and deal with his suspension.

He picked up his bookbag, looked down at the caterpillar one more time, and as he lifted his foot to start his walk home, he bent his knee up higher, and slammed his foot down on the pavement ... killing the caterpillar.

CHAPTER 8

ater that evening, after dinner, Kris and Tony were cuddled up on the couch. He began kissing the back of her neck, his hand sliding from her back to her waist and then to her breasts. Without saying a word, they walked back to the bedroom, and she sat on the edge of the bed. Tony, still kissing her as he slowly undressed her.

Kris laid down on the bed and moved over so he could climb in bed with her. She was completely nude and felt very vulnerable to the point of feeling uncomfortable. Kris was never extremely comfortable having sex with her partners and did not like for them to see her nude. It was not because of the rape but because she had felt that way since her first sexual experience. It did not have anything to do with not having good sex either, or that she felt unsafe with her partners, she just could never get past a feeling of awkwardness around them.

Tony was lightly rubbing his fingers down the length of Kris's body. Kissing each spot he touched, his hand made its way down to her thigh and he gently grasped underneath her knee, bending it up and towards him.

As his fingers traced the inside of her thigh, Kris's mind went in a completely different direction.

The image in Kris's mind went to the memory of an encounter she had with a friend of hers and it had suddenly flooded back to her. The encounter happened when Kris and Tony were trying to "enhance" their marriage and became a part of a swinger's community. Their involvement started a couple of years before this encounter.

Now in 7th Grade, Mack had changed quite a bit. He had continued to deal with comments and name calling since that day in the gym. When he got home from school on the day he was suspended, his parents were dumbfounded. He was pretty sure his father had suspicions about his son, because when Mack was telling his parents his side of the events, his father exploded with rage. Now, Mack worked very hard at becoming more of a "man.". At 13, he lifted weights, and he started playing sports.

It was Texas, so of course he was on the football team for the town. He really liked playing baseball when he wasn't playing football, and if he had any "spare" time, he spent it with his girlfriend. There was not much dating going on because they were only 13. Mack would walk her down the hall to class, carry her bookbag, and they'd meet at a local hangout, which was a small restaurant in town. One of his classmates' moms worked there, so she would call any of the boy's parents if they got out of line.

Another way Mack had changed—he no longer broke up fights, he usually started them. His victims were usually younger and "nerdier." The best part for Mack was he had help in his new endeavors. His new partner in crime was none other than Jake. The two boys, when not playing ball, were engaging in reckless behavior on their bikes because they weren't old enough to drive. Jake also had a girlfriend, but neither boy had done anything other than kiss the girls on the cheek. Jack and Mack were riding their bikes to the hangout, talking about their girlfriends and how the other boys boasted about kissing girls, the REAL way.

Mack asked, "Do you really think Jamie touched Sammy's boobs?"

"No. Do you?" Jake asked.

"I don't know. Maybe he just brushed his hand against it and counted that as 'touching.'"

"Have you touched Grace's?"

"I tried but she slapped my hand hard. She is lucky I didn't hit her back."

"Don't do that. That will get you in trouble."

"Well, how am I supposed to get her to let me touch them?"

"I will help you think of something," Mack told him.

"What do you mean?" Jake asked.

"Alcohol makes people tired. Maybe you could put alcohol in her soda. She will go to sleep and then you can do it," Mack told him.

"I think she would smell it."

"Let's have a party then. Maybe she will drink if she sees everyone else doing it."

Jake thought about it for a minute. "That is not a half bad idea Mack. Why haven't you done that with Wendy?"

"Oh, I will. I am just waiting for the right time," Mack said, the entire time knowing he would

HAVE *to do something with Wendy and provide proof. He was still being called names, but not nearly as much since he had been bulking up and teamed up with Jake. He was still somewhat smaller than the other boys in class, so when there were enough of them, and Mack was alone, he was still being tormented.*

As the boys sat with their girlfriends at the restaurant, Mack put his hand on Wendy's knee.

He slowly crept his hand up her thigh. When he reached a certain point, she clenched her legs closed and scooted away from him a little. It was then that Mack decided he would not be rejected by anyone, especially a girl. He put his hand back on her knee and squeezed hard enough to make her wince. He looked at her and made sure she was looking back at him.

When he knew she was looking, he darted his eyes down to her legs, pointing his index finger out, indicating he wanted her to part her legs again.

Slowly, Wendy complied. His hand went back up her thigh, finding its way to where he wanted to touch. Well, she likes me, he thought, despite his not reacting physically to what he was doing to her. He drew his hand back, looking at her like it was her fault. She put her head down and did not say another word. When her mom came to pick her up, Wendy leaned in to hug Mack, and he whispered in her ear, "Next time I want more."

He eventually got more. There were a couple of occasions where he fondled her, including when he and Jake had their party. They waited until Mack's parents went out of town to have the party because Mack would be alone in the house. His younger sister went with their parents on a week-long trip. There were about 10 boys and their girlfriends at the house. Jake and Mack spiked the drinks with vodka. The taste was "off" to the girls, but everyone complained about it. One of the boys on the team started giving Mack trouble. "Geez Mack, I have heard your kind know how to cook and do hair. You can't even pour punch without it tasting like shit."

Wendy laughed at the boy, partially because she was drunk and partially because the comment had clearly upset him.

At this point, the fight was on. It lasted about three minutes with fists flying and nasty comments being hurled. "I bet you still can't get your dick hard with girls. I bet you dream about Coach for that."

Wendy jumped in "Mack, please stop! You are going to get in trouble again."

Mack stood up and told the boy to leave, which he gladly did. Wendy continued to drink until she could barely stand up. She was very loose, and this was Mack's opportunity to make his move. He got Jake's attention, and the two boys, Grace and Wendy went upstairs to Mack's room. The four of them were in the room, the door shut and all of them sat on the edge of Mack's bed.

Jake started kissing Grace and he put his hand on her breast. This time she did not resist or stop him, as she had so many times before. He immediately responded to his actions. At the other end of the bed, Mack was doing the same thing, but occasionally, he would look over at Jake, imagining what it would be like to kiss him instead of Wendy. When the thought popped into his head, he began to react physically. The kissing and fondling continued for both couples, Mack indicated to Wendy that he wanted her to touch him. She wouldn't comply, which instantly upset him. Mack stood up, and positioned himself in front of Wendy, but he was still able to see Jake. "I said touch it," he told her. When she started to extend her shaking hand, Mack grabbed her wrist and said, "Wait." And with his other hand, he unbuttoned and unzipped his jeans. "Since you wouldn't touch it with your hand, now you can put your mouth on it."

Jake and Grace stopped what they were doing and turned to look at Mack and Wendy. Jake leaned over and whispered something in her ear. She got up and left the room. "Mack, I don't know what you want me to do," Wendy said through slow tears.

"Put your mouth on it and suck like you would suck through a straw," he told her.

Jake spoke up, "I am going to leave you alone, Mack."

"No! Stay here so you can tell everyone I am not a fag like they keep saying I am." Mack pointed to Jake's groin. "It doesn't look like you are either. Take it out, and she can do you too."

It wasn't too much longer before Mack finished, and not because of what Wendy was doing to him, but because in his mind, it was Jake doing it. Mack told Wendy to do Jake too, but Jake had changed his mind and left the room, got Grace from downstairs, and walked her home.

What Mack didn't realize, was that Jake caught Mack watching him occasionally. Not long after this, Jake made himself scarce, finding other people to hang with and was sure to tell the other boys on their team what Mack did, including the part about Mack watching him and Grace, with most of the attention being paid to Jake than Grace.

CHAPTER 9

Tony and Kris had just moved into their home and one October night, Kris was talking to a mutual military friend in a chat room. She privately messaged Kris and told her she needed to look up a profile on an adult swinger's website. When she did, Kris intuitively knew it was Tony's profile. Initially the discovery and following discussion was very heated, mostly on Kris's end because she had already caught Tony talking to other women, setting up meetings with them, and making plans to meet them behind Kris's back. To her knowledge, Tony had not cheated on her physically at this point.

Once Kris was a little calmer, she asked Tony, "What would you have done had I created a profile and didn't tell you about it?" To which he replied he did not care one way or the other. He had encouraged Kris to create a profile and explained that he wanted to add some excitement to the marriage.

One night, while Tony was working overnight on the ship, Kris made her profile and entered a chat room for people who lived in Virginia and Maryland. She chatted for a little while, sitting back, and watching the conversations. One couple advertised a "Meet and Greet" at a local bar/restaurant called Cowboy Bar and Grille. When asked if she would be there, Kris made her excuses about the upcoming event. When Tony came home the following morning, she told him about the chat room and the event.

"Are you going to go?" he asked.

"I don't know. Are you going to go with me?"

"I have a deployment coming up remember. I will be gone for a couple of months babe."

Kris thought about it for a moment. "I don't like going places alone, at least where I don't know anybody," she told Tony.

"Isn't that the point? You are going there to meet people and greet them. Thus, a meet and greet," he said as he laughed.

She playfully slapped him on the arm. "We haven't even really talked about this. Are there rules, guidelines? I have no clue how this works. You are the one that worked at a swinger's club in San Diego when you were a young pup."

"Well, swinger's clubs are a little bit different. I don't think you will be able to walk around the Cowboy without clothing. It would be interesting to be sure. Oh, I know, we can get you a pair of assless chaps!"

"Buddy, you are pushing it with me." Kris laughed. "Seriously, how do YOU want this to work? Do you want me to go by myself? What happens if I meet the man of my dreams? What if …"

"Or woman, you never know." Tony said only half kidding. Kris was not aware, but Tony originally set up a profile on the site to see if she would engage sexually with other women. He had a feeling for a while now that Kris was not living her truth.

He loved her and he knew she loved him, but she was still very reserved sexually with him. She didn't like him to see her naked. She never repelled from his touch, but he could feel her tenseness. Sure, some of that may have been from the childhood abuse and from the past rape, but she had not always remembered that.

Tony wanted to see how Kris would react to the suggestion of adding a third person, preferably a woman, to the bedroom. They had discussed it earlier in their marriage, but it was a one-sided discussion and Kris was having none of it. She had gotten offended when he suggested it. Now, it seemed, she was a little warmer to the idea. When they discussed entering into the lifestyle this time, Kris could not help but wonder if Tony was cheating on her, because he was so willing to let her be with other men.

"I'm not interested in another woman," she told him. What she really was not sure of was the possibility of not only another person seeing her naked, but that other person being a woman.

"Well, if we add a third person, I would like for it to be a woman. I don't really want to cross swords," he said.

"Great analogy Tony. If we are going to get involved in this, there must be some ground rules."

"Okay, how about this. If you want to find someone else when I am out on deployments, I am okay with that. I want you to get comfortable with it all, and we can talk about what to do if there is a third involved."

"Tony, we have been married long enough that you know damn good and well, I am not going to be okay with you being alone with another female. How is that fair to you?"

"Do not worry about me. I will follow your lead. I want you to go to one of those meet and greets and do some recon. See what is out there, what the swinger community is like. Then report back to me."

"Oh sure, make me do all the work again. How typical of you," she said as she rolled her eyes at him. "So, are we going to look for a couple to switch partners with? An individual to join us? What do YOU want?" Kris asked him.

"I would prefer a single female or a female from a couple that is allowed to play alone, but with us, if that makes sense. Do you want to be with another man with me around?"

"Not particularly, no. Yes, that did make sense the way you worded it. So, a threesome with me and another female is your preference?"

"Yes. Is that okay?" he asked.

"I have my reservations. I don't know how that will work either. Am I going to be a part of it or just sitting off to the side?"

Tony held her hands, "I would really like for you to be a part of it. I think it will be sensual… no, make that really flipping hot!" He sounded like a kid at Christmas.

"I will try. I am not going to make any promises Tony. We tried this twice before, and I wasn't really into it. It was weird and uncomfortable. It isn't going to be someone from your work again, is it? I would prefer it wasn't someone we have known for a long time and honestly, your choices were not the greatest, so I get to choose this time."

He laughed, "Fair enough. I am sure you can find someone who does not have 'man hands' too."

"Ugh, yeah, that was REALLY awkward, and kind of nasty," she said.

"I am so sorry about that. Seriously Kris, I want you to go to a meet and greet and see if this is something you want to do."

CHAPTER 10

Ronnie contacted Penelope to update her on what she had found in the investigation up to this point. "Well, this certainly may be a game changer for Kris. I need to have my investigator, John, look into this a little more as well. Thank you, Ronnie, it will certainly be interesting to see how this all plays out."

Kris and Tony were doing the best they could with life. Things were very tense between them, and Kris couldn't go anywhere because of the ankle bracelet. On top of it all, she was fairly sure Tony was having another affair. The worst part was, there was no way to catch him. It was just Kris being paranoid. Then again, every time she was paranoid, she was right. It could also be the stress she was under while waiting for her trial to start.

Each time she had spoken to Ronnie, she was told there was nothing new in the investigation to report. It did not look good from what Kris could tell. She became more depressed as the date of her trial drew near. This was Kris's favorite time of the year, mostly because it was Halloween. It was almost mid-October and ironically enough, her trial was starting the same week as Halloween. This year, she was going to miss being able to take part in it. One of her friends had a birthday close to Halloween and always threw a big party, and another would set up tables with food and snacks in her garage while the kids went Trick-or-Treating. Everyone who came brought a dish and drinks and dressed up. '*I guess I can always go in black and white striped pajamas*' Kris thought to herself, trying to lighten the severity of what she was really going to be doing for Halloween.

There was a flight back to St. Louis mid-week before the trial. Tony scheduled a flight the same day so he could be there with her. Kris was going to be allowed to stay with her mom and dad, so that was comforting. They were helping her with attorney fees as well. Penelope was an extremely good attorney, but Kris was still not feeling great about the situation. She wanted a little information, something to give her a little hope. To her understanding, Ronnie was still working on the case for Penelope, but the department did not know. Kris didn't doubt it if Terry was also helping Ronnie and Penelope at this point.

The phone rang, and it was Penelope. "Hey Kris, how are you doing?"

"I am okay. Getting a little down and don't know how to get out of this funk. I can talk to Adrienne but even that is not helping at this point."

"Do not give up, Kris. If you're getting too depressed, are you able to get your doctor to prescribe you something?"

"I really don't want to be on anything. I haven't been able to find anything that doesn't make me feel like a zombie or worse than how I feel right now."

"Well, you know better than anyone what is going to work for you Kris. Just promise me that if it gets too bad, you will do something."

"Of course, Penelope. So, have you decided about putting me on the stand?"

"I can tell you that I would advise against it. If you are going to insist on it, there is nothing I can do about it."

"Can we see how things are going before I make that decision?" Kris asked.

"Yes, of course, but I am still going to caution you against it. Prosecution is going to be brutal with witnesses as it is. You know this. I don't want them going at you twice as hard. I know you did not do this Kris, but right now they have an incredibly good motive for you to HAVE done it."

"Yes, they do. Most of the evidence is circumstantial though, right? My nightstick had been missing, and I didn't even know it until Ronnie and Terry asked for it."

"It is mostly circumstantial, yes, but they will make the argument that you dumped it, thus the tampering charge." Penelope said.

"I know. I am just looking for something to hold onto at this point. Ronnie keeps telling me she isn't any further in the investigation, and you haven't said anything about John having progressed either. I'm kind of tired of feeling like I am in the dark with this. This is my LIFE that we are talking about. I would much prefer to not be spending it behind bars."

"Kris, I know this is asking a lot, but I really need you to be patient. Ronnie and John are both working hard at tracking some leads down. Until these become more concrete, I don't want to go into detail. Just PLEASE trust us."

"I am trying Penelope. I really am. I really am feeling like I am in the dark and have no control. Not having control or a say in this is making my anxiety go through the roof."

"I completely understand, Kris. You have trusted Ronnie in the past, just know she and I have everything under control. Just keep trusting us. I know it is easier said than done, but I promise you, we aren't going to do anything to make you NOT trust us. I also wanted to let you know, I will be on the flight with you as the police escort you into St. Louis. I have talked to the detectives and the judge, and all have agreed that it won't be necessary to handcuff you. The ankle monitor is enough, and we don't want to draw any attention to you. We will be there in the morning on the Wednesday before the trial and leave that Thursday. That should give you some time to rest before the trial."

"Oh, that's great news. A mini vacay to sleep in a bed with a door and not bars," Kris said with sarcasm and venom in her voice.

Penelope ignored the anger coming from Kris. She knew it was all coming from a place of fear more than anything. She was doing all she could to reassure Kris, but it wasn't working. Penelope knew Kris's need for answers, but until the information being investigated became solid, she didn't want to tell Kris.

Two weeks before the trial started, Penelope was in her office going through all her notes when her phone rang. It was Ronnie. "Hey Ronnie, what do you have?"

"I found Elaine. She left town quite some time ago after quitting her practice. According to her, Mack had been threatening her and her mother if she ever testified to what Kris disclosed about the rape."

"But why? The statute of limitations was up for filing criminal charges, and Kris decided not to go through with a civil suit."

"I don't think Mack knew that though. I know where Shaen is too, but you will have to have John call because he knows me from his time with St. Louis Police."

"That's not a problem. I can get John on that today. Let's get back to Elaine. Are you looking into her whereabouts during the time of Mack's time of death? Any indication she was out of town during that period?"

"If she was, I haven't found it yet. She most certainly had a reason to kill Mack, as much as anyone else does. Unfortunately, Kris has the biggest motive of all. Hell, if I would have had the chance …"

"DON'T SAY IT!!! I already know. I don't need to defend both of you. The good news in all of this, there is an exceptionally lengthy list of people who could have done this. Mack sure did make some enemies along the way, didn't he?"

"Yes, he did. He was arrogant," Ronnie said. "He used his dad's position in the department to manipulate other people and get what he wanted. I am quite sure by doing that, it made a lot of people mad. As for Shaen he continued his behaviors too."

"What do you mean?" she asked Ronnie.

Ronnie told Penelope of instances she was told about by people from the police department Shaen currently works for. "Some of the things he did were as a patrol officer, both in the city and in the current police department, but mostly with the current police department because he had more opportunities to do so. When he was a detective, and working a prostitution sting, he used his position, or attempted to do so in this case, to try and coerce sexual favors from a woman at the hotel who was not there as a prostitute," Ronnie said as she continued the story.

"The woman in question was at the hotel with her then fiancé, and admittedly they were getting ready to use some illicit narcotic when detectives opened the door. She was not a prostitute when the hotel was raided, never has been, but when Shaen and other officers went into the room to search, they found the drugs.

The woman relayed to me that Shaen took the situation and ran with it. He pulled the woman to his lap and began groping her in front of her fiancé. She told me that is when Shaen offered to make the drug charges go away if she had sex with him."

"So, what happened?" Penelope asked.

"She and her fiancé both took the charges. She knew the truth and admitted that she was there with her fiancé to use, but that was the extent. Now, they are married and have kids, a home, excellent jobs, and have stayed out of trouble."

"Will she come forward about this voluntarily?"

"I don't know. She seemed nervous talking to me. She knows Shaen is still in the department and doesn't want him to be able to retaliate. I can understand why you want her to come forward though. It will show that Kris isn't the only one to have grudges and puts Shaen in the hotseat. "

"The problem with putting Shaen in the hotseat at this point is, we don't have anything to show cause as a reason for HIM to want Mack dead," Penelope said. "Mack wasn't connected to the woman and her husband. Only with Kris."

"Sure, you do. Mack was the only one brought in for the questioning of Kris's rape. She didn't even remember Shaen's name until after she tried to file charges. Mack knew that and would have had no problem using it to blackmail Shaen. I found the phone records showing all the calls between the two from the time Kris filed charges until the possible day Mack was killed. There were a LOT of them Penelope, and it was mostly Mack calling Shaen. I can assure you that Mack was a big enough asshole to blackmail someone and make sure he didn't go down alone."

"Did you get both of their phone records?"

"Yes," Ronnie replied.

"Anything of significance?"

CHAPTER 11

A couple of weeks later, Kris was sitting at the computer and began chatting on the adult site. The couple she had been talking to in the chat room mentioned another meet and greet. She said she wasn't sure about going and a private message popped up. It was the wife, and she told Kris that the meet and greets were a no-expectation gathering. Just because people attended did not mean they were obligated to go home with someone. "We would love to meet you," the woman said. "We do this meet and greet every Tuesday, and it is a good way to get out and just relax for the evening and be around other adults."

Kris finally relented. She got up from the computer, took a quick shower and got ready. *What do I even wear? I don't know if I am supposed to dress up, wear what I normally do – I don't know if I can do this* she said to herself. *I hate going out alone, but like Tony said, that is the point of this. And I don't have to have sex with everyone I meet.* After an hour of talking herself in and out of going, she finally grabbed her keys and drove to the meet and greet. The woman told Kris what she would be wearing so she could find her easily. When Kris arrived, she sat in the parking lot, a packed parking lot, and psyched herself up again.

She walked into the restaurant and noticed a large crowd around the bar and seating area. She scanned the room, looking for a woman wearing a black tank top and leather jacket. She told Kris she had long, straight brown hair with some lighter streaks throughout. After scanning the room for a minute or more and not spotting the woman, she started to turn around and leave when Kris heard her chat name being called out.

Kris turned back around and saw a woman who was slightly shorter than her. She looked exactly as she described herself, but she left something out. As Kris watched her approach, she noticed the woman's piercing eyes. They were mesmerizing and instantly drew Kris in. The woman reached her hand out to shake Kris's "Hello, I'm Tess. It is so nice to finally meet you." As Kris took her hand, she could feel the heat from Tess. Kris also felt an electricity in her that she had never experienced *before. She could not explain it to herself, but it sparked something in her physically and eventually told herself it was the nervousness of meeting new people, especially for a purpose as specific as this.*

Shaen lay in bed, pretending to be asleep as the bedroom door opened. He closed his eyes tighter and didn't have to guess who was coming in. He could smell the cheap aftershave on his uncle's face. "Shaen, are you asleep or pretending to be asleep?"

Shaen didn't stir. He thought if he didn't move, his uncle would leave the room. He was wrong. His uncle sat on the side of the bed and reached under the covers. He began to rub Shaen all over his lower body. He slid his hand down the front of Shaen's pajama pants and underwear, rubbing his penis. Shaen began to react, his body responding in a way he begged for it not to. As his erection started, his uncle began stroking himself with his other hand.

"I know you are awake now, Shaen. "Look at me. I want you to look at my penis." Shaen did not open his eyes. "Shaen, you can open them, or I can find a way to make you open them."

He complied with his uncle's demand. "Good boy. I knew you weren't really sleeping. You know the rule, right?"

"Yes."

"What is the rule?" his uncle asked him.

"Don't tell anyone or you will hurt Jamie." Jamie was Shaen's twin brother.

"That's right. That means you will do whatever I want you to, right?"

"Yes," Shaen said timidly.

"Good. Now look at my penis."

Shaen did as he was told as his uncle continued to stroke himself. "Take your pajamas off."

Shaen hesitated, and his uncle quickly noticed it. "Do it now Shaen." He said as he gripped Shaen's scrotum. Shaen quickly took off his pajamas and underwear. "There you go. That will be much easier now. Get on your hands and knees so I can put this in your mouth."

Once again, he did as he was told and while he was being forced to do this, his uncle reached over Shaen's head and shoved two fingers into Shaen. As soon as his uncle was repeatedly penetrating Shaen, he ejaculated in Shaen's mouth. "Don't throw up. If you do, someone will hear you, and Jamie will be the one to pay for it." Shaen began to cry, but silently. He did not want his brother to endure the same things he had been enduring for the last few months.

When it finally stopped for the night, and his uncle was leaving the room, Shaen heard his mom walking down the hall and address her brother. "Please tell me you did not do anything to him."

"And what if I did? What are you going to do about it?"

"Have you not hurt enough people? You are the reason Jimmy did what he did. I will not have the same thing happened to my boys. You need help. You have been doing this for far too long."

"And again, sis, what are YOU going to do about it?" There was silence from Shaen's mother.

"That is what I thought." Her brother said as he walked down the stairs.

'What is happening here?' Shaen thought. Why isn't she telling dad? She knows what he is doing, and she hasn't told anyone? Shaen instantly became angry with his mother. He vowed to himself that he would never forgive her. She did nothing to stop this, and not only did she not do anything about that night, but she allowed the abuse to continue for years. It finally stopped when Shaen was 16. By then he was able to drive, work, and escape from home, even if it was just for a little while. He had also started to drink, and he did so in secret. Much of his life had been about secrets, so this became very natural for him. He was very good at hiding what he did—or so he thought.

Shaen came home from a school function much later than he was told to be home, walking in the house as quietly as he could but was failing at doing so. The less noise he attempted to make, the more he made. He did not want to wake his parents, but it didn't matter, his mother was already sitting in the living room on the couch when he came in. On the table in front of her were empty alcohol bottles.

"What is going on with you Shaen?" The smell of the alcohol he had been drinking suddenly hit her nose.

"You're DRUNK," she said in a loud whisper and then looked down the hall to see if anyone was coming.

"No shit Mom."

"Don't you dare talk to me that way."

"What exactly are you going to do about it?"

"I am going to go get your father up. We all need to have a talk." She pointed at the bottles on the table and said, "Obviously this is something you do quite a bit. Why? I don't understand." She started to stand up, and Shaen moved to stand in front of her.

"You aren't going to go tell Dad anything."

"Yes, I am, now move out of my way."

"You aren't."

"Shaen, your father and I love you very much, and he needs to know about this so we can get you some help."

"Oh, NOW you want to help me? NOW?!?!" he yelled. "You sure as FUCK didn't want to help when Uncle Tim was in my room every time he came over to visit. Did you think he was just coming in to say goodbye? No, you KNEW what he was doing."

"Oh, Baby Boy, I had no idea." She said, hoping he believed her.

"Yeah Mom, you did have an idea. I heard you outside the door one night talking to him about Uncle Jimmy, and that he better not be 'doing the same thing you did to Jimmy.'"

"You need to keep your voice down so your father doesn't hear you."

"Wow, what are you protecting HIM from? You were supposed to be protecting me and Jamie, but I was the one who protected him. I did whatever Uncle Tim wanted so he wouldn't go anywhere near my brother. So, Mom, you are NOT going to tell Dad anything. You don't get to pick and choose when you are going to be a parent and be protective. That boat sailed a long time ago."

She sat back down, and tears began to stream from her face. "I am so sorry, Shaen. I don't know what to say."

"There is nothing for you to say, and I do not need an apology from you. What I do need now is for you to buy my alcohol and you aren't going to tell dad because if you do, I am going to tell him what happened to me and that you knew the entire time. I would guess that won't make him very happy."

After that night, Shaen's relationship with his parents was distant at best, especially with his mom. Of course, he loved his parents but had no use for any unnecessary contact. Once he graduated from high school, he, and his brother both went off to college. They stuck together most of the time at school, went on double dates, and shared a dorm room.

Jamie was much timider than Shaen. Shaen was very cocky and arrogant and did not take "no" for an answer. The difference between him and Mack, was that Shaen didn't use drugs to get what he wanted, he gained leverage over the people he wanted something from and blackmailed them. It did not have to be a female for him to use it either, but a woman was the easiest target for him.

CHAPTER 12

Mack was sitting in his biology class and watching the other student walking in. His current girlfriend, Debbie, walked through the door and was wearing Mack's football jersey. He still played, despite the continuous hazing by his teammates. He also continued to work out and was more muscular than he had ever been. He had grown into any awkwardness he displayed in his younger years, so much so that their biology teacher, Samantha Neylan, also took notice. The age gap between the two was not that great. She was a first-year teacher but had graduated earlier than some of her college classmates.

Mack knew she watched him, and he knew why. He knew he was good looking, and he couldn't blame her for watching him. I would pay attention to me too, he thought to himself. As Debbie sat down; she saw Mack watching the teacher. "Hey! Stop it!" she said loudly.

"Stop what?"

"Stop watching who you are watching," she replied through gritted teeth.

"What do you care? It's not like you are interested in me, and she is."

"I am dating you, aren't I?"

"You know what I am talking about Debbie."

"I am not doing it Mack. I am not ready. Besides, you don't love me, you are only dating me because it makes you look good. I have seen the way you look at other girls." Debbie left off the rest of what she was thinking because he looked at them as though they were diseased. She really wasn't sure why he wanted to have sex with her because she was pretty sure he did not like girls AT ALL.

Debbie was a cheerleader and had watched Mack on the sidelines quite a bit. There was one time after a play, as he was coming off the field, the coach patted Mack's butt which was quite common in men's sports for some reason. When the coach did that, Mack turned red and looked at the coach the way she wished he would look at her.

"If you won't then I will find someone who will," he said.

"Fine by me!" Debbie replied. With that said, she took off Mack's jersey and threw it at him.

The entire class, including Ms. Neylan, instantly became quiet. Mack's face turned red and purple with anger. She just made the biggest mistake of her life, Mack thought to himself. Later that week, Mack went and apologized to Debbie, brought her flowers, and asked her to the homecoming dance. She finally agreed, and that is when he started setting his plan into motion.

The dance was on a Saturday night, and the Homecoming game was on the Friday before. Mack made a phone call to one of his friends who lived on a horse ranch. "Hey, were you able to get that stuff for me?"

"Yeah, but you don't own horses, what do you need it for?"

"I am doing a research project for the science fair. I read somewhere that it can be used for people too, and I want to see the effects and aftereffects it has on me at different doses."

"Dude, you better be careful. It can really fuck you up."

"I will be. Trust me, I do not want to fry my brain or anything."

"Okay. I will bring it in my gym bag tonight."

A smile spread across Mack's face. "That is perfect. Thanks man. I owe you big. See you tonight."

A couple of hours later, Mack walked into the school and down to the locker room to get ready for the game. When he opened his locker, there was a pair of pink ballet shoes hanging where his cleats would be. In place of his pants and pads, there was a tutu. His game jersey had white medical tape on the back over his last name that read "Twinkletoes," and there was a note taped to the jersey— "The new uniform for Twinkletoes." His face turned purple with anger for the second time in a week. He ripped everything from the hooks, removed the tape, and balled it up.

A few of the teammates were in the corner of the locker room, snickering and looking at Mack.

He took off a regular tennis shoe and threw it at the group in the corner. This elicited a fight among the players when one of the boys went rushing at Mack. At the same time, Mack went rushing at the entire group. They had not been close friends in a long time, but much to his surprise, Jake was among the group of boys in the melee. The coach, who had the blinds closed in his office as he was going over the playbook for the night, heard the ruckus from behind his door. He ran out, and his yelling stopped everyone in their tracks or mid-swing. "What in the actual FUCK is going on?!"

"Those assholes put ballet shit in my locker with this!" he said as he grabbed the note and handed it to the coach.

"Who did this? Tell me NOW, or I will go out to the field and tell the officials and the other team we forfeit this game because I DON'T HAVE A TEAM!"

Three of the boys stepped forward, including Jake, and said they had done it together. "Thank you, boys, for being adult enough to come forward … you are all benched."

"BUT COACH." They started to protest.

Through gritted teeth, "Not. One. More. Word. ALL of you, give me your jerseys. You have not earned the right to wear these tonight. Not even from the sidelines."

The group of boys handed over their jerseys. "Parkins, in my office first."

Mack walked in with his head down. He did not dare look at the coach because he knew something would be said by his teammates, and that was the last thing he needed right now. As he walked by the others, he heard Jake telling the rest of the group, "He is always staring at us when we are getting dressed."

Another of the boys mumbled at Mack, "Fucking faggot."

I will show them all I am not gay, especially Debbie, he thought.

When the coach came into the office and closed the door, Mack had to distract his mind from the situation to keep from physically reacting to being alone in the coach's office with the door closed. As the coach talked, he barely heard a word because he was thinking about what was going to happen during the dance the following night, and how he was going to get Debbie alone.

Debbie woke up Sunday morning feeling like she had been hit by one of the school buses. She felt like she had been sweating overnight but couldn't understand why. It had been a nice night, so, the windows were open for the fresh air to come into the house. What was even weirder, is

her clothes were only damp on her pajama bottoms. Still groggy, she rolled out of bed, grabbed her towel from the back of her bedroom door and walked down the hall to the bathroom. Her parents had gone to church but let her sleep in because the dance went so late.

She looked in the mirror and saw darkness around her eyes, not comprehending her eye was a little swollen and the darkness was bruising and not her eye make-up she hadn't washed off when she got home. The truth was, she didn't remember much beyond the Homecoming Court King and Queen announcement. She remembered Mack getting them a snack and a soda and then taking a walk outside to get some fresh air. With all the students and the dancing, it had gotten hot in the gym. She could not remember anything after going outside.

She still hadn't put two and two together until she took her pajama pants off and looked once more into the mirror, seeing hickies on her breasts. There was no way she would have let Mack do that. Maybe we were in an accident, and it is from a seatbelt. I will have to call Mack and find out, she thought. She was stepping out of her pajama pants and underwear and found the source of her sweating—it was blood, and it was at the front and back of her underwear.

CHAPTER 13

Ronnie began going over the frequent calls from both Mack and Shaen. Based on what she was relaying to Penelope, there were frequent calls from Mack's phone, not just to Shaen, but to others in Kris's life—friends, family, former and current co-workers, and professors. Shaen had numerous incoming calls from Mack as well as a number that Ronnie was still trying to track down.

"Here is the thing. One number shows up multiple times on both phones, and I haven't been able to attach it to anyone." Ronnie explained.

"Who has the most calls with the number?" Penelope asked.

"Shaen. The calls stop to both phones, outgoing and incoming about a week after Mack was found, which makes sense with Mack's phone, but not with Shaen's. As I look closer, the calls stop to Shaen before they do to Mack."

"If you can track down the number, can you try to get records to that as well?"

"I will work on it. I tried calling it, but it is disconnected now," Ronnie Mentioned.

"Is there anything else important?"

"I have found some other victims of Mack's. One is still an officer in the city, but she was out of state for a training seminar and there were no calls from her phone to Mack or Shaen and they didn't call her. Like Kris, the other two left the department not too long after their incidents. They live out of state and their whereabouts are also accounted for."

"So, this mystery number may be our key? And is it possible any of them bought a "throw-away" phone to make contact?"

Ronnie paused for a second before she answered. "Well, yes, it's very possible. If it is a "throw-away," it's really going to be hard to track, but I will do my best."

"Let's just hope something comes up soon. I'd like to have as much as possible going into the trial. Kris is getting really discouraged, and that is partially on me. I didn't want to tell her too much of what we have and the leads you and John are working on, because if she knows and the information doesn't pan out, I am terrified her mood will get worse."

"I know," Ronnie responded. "I am really worried about her. I am just thankful she can be at her parents' house before and during her trial. I am not sure how it happened to work that way but thank God for HUGE favors."

"You don't think she will do something stupid do you? You know her better than most of us, but she doesn't strike me as someone who will hurt herself. Then again, most people can be surprising."

Ronnie thought for a second and responded to Penelope with some hesitance. "I don't THINK Kris would hurt herself, but every time I talk to her, she is more and more disconnected. I will reach out to Adrienne and see what she thinks. She won't tell me much because of HIPPA laws, but I can at the very least, let her know we are worried and ask her to reach out to Kris."

"Good idea. If you need me to do the same, let me know. For now, I am going to work on some strategies and go through work and personal histories for Shaen and Mack. Oh, I have John looking into this too, but could you find out if this has just been a "Mack and Shaen" event or if Mack had other rookies doing this before and after Shaen came onto the department?"

"Absolutely. I know a few people who were trained by Mack. It would be interesting to see what the dynamics were like between him and the females he trained."

"Ronnie, I don't know why that never occurred to me. Looking at the males he trained is smart, but THAT is even smarter."

Ronnie laughed a little and said, "Yeah, well, having police friends in the LGBT community provides a little insight. Some of the stories I have heard from them are enough to try the patience of a saint. Straight or gay, women in police work really deal with a lot of shit. Kris is living proof of that, and he didn't even train her."

"I wonder if that may be our mystery call. Get back to me as soon as you can please. I don't care what time of day or night it is, the moment you get some info, call me."

"I sure will Penelope." Ronnie hung up the phone. She called Trixie to let her know she needed to make some phone calls and a couple of stops before coming home.

"How is Kris doing?" Trixie asked.

"Well, that is one of the calls I need to make." Ronnie told Trixie about Kris's increasingly sour mood, about the depression and defeat she hears from Kris any time she or Penelope talks to her. "I'm just so worried about her, and so is Penelope. I'm going to call her therapist and see if she will reach out to her."

"This is why I love you, Ronnie. You are so compassionate and aware of other people's feelings. You have a genuine concern and care for others that enough people in your line of work don't have anymore. I love you, and I will see you in a while."

"I love you too and will be home as soon as I can." Ronnie's next call was to Adrienne. "Hello Adrienne, this is Ronnie Lowell. I am a friend and former co-worker of Kris …"

"You don't even have to finish," Adrienne said. "Kris has talked about you quite frequently during our sessions, and I am afraid that is all I can say at this point. She is still under my care and of course, I am sure you know our conversations are privileged and confidential."

"Oh, yes ma'am, I know that. I am calling to let you know both her attorney and I are very worried about her right now, and we were wondering if you would be willing to reach out to her. We know she won't reach out herself, given all she is dealing with at the moment."

"I can absolutely do that. Do you mind elaborating on her mental health status so I can make some notes?"

Ronnie began telling Adrienne about Kris's declining mood and how defeated and distant Kris was when talking to her.

She told Adrienne she did not think Kris would harm herself, but that Kris was well resigned to the fact that she would be going to prison for murdering Mack. Adrienne was making notes as Ronnie described

Kris's current mood. Adrienne had already begun making plans to testify at the trial but decided that she would fly a couple of days earlier to sit down with Kris and gauge where she was mentally. They had worked together for so long that Kris was unable to "fake" moods with Adrienne. Adrienne was usually surprisingly good at figuring out when Kris was hiding something from her. She told Ronnie of her plans and asked her to let Penelope know as well. Ronnie agreed and the two hung up.

CHAPTER 14

*T*he night went very well, and over the next few weeks Kris attended Tuesday evening gatherings as often as she could. She was developing friendships with Tess and others. Most of the people attending the meet and greets were couples with a few singles mixed in here and there. Kris had also met a couple of single men through the site, and one she had meetings with more than once. Tony was fully aware of these meetings and asked only that Kris be safe. The man Kris had been meeting was younger, well-built and was able to make Kris feel comfortable in her own skin, as much as that was possible for her.

She would see him at least once a week for a while, but eventually he ended up moving. Mostly, Kris enjoyed going out with Tess and other ladies she met through the Tuesday night gatherings. When Tony returned from his deployment, he would go with her, but they had not "hooked up" with anyone from the group. They did do quite a bit with the people they had become friends and attended family gatherings, barbeques, and birthday parties.

Tess and her husband were allowed to be with another partner on an individual basis. They did not have the rule of playing together, and in fact, Tess's husband preferred being with someone without Tess involved. Tess was okay with being alone with someone or with a couple.

One of the first encounters with Tess took place after a birthday party. Tony and Kris ended up taking Tess home from the restaurant the party was held at because Tess's husband was being hateful, and she wanted to leave. Tess had parked her car at their house and when they all got home, Tess and Kris started kissing. One thing led to another and the three of them ended up in bed together. It was an amazing and extremely sensual experience for Kris, one she hoped would be repeated. After that evening, Kris would go to Tess's house during the day when Tess had a group of women over for a "girl's day," eating lunch, swimming, and sitting in the hot tub. These days usually involved some sexual play as well.

As Tony was doing the same things, all Kris could think about was Tess. She remembered the tenderness and sensuality of the encounter that eventually turned into a long night of lovemaking. Kris enjoyed being with Tess. She was gentle and patient with Kris. Despite having been with a woman before, Kris was still "green" and at times, was not sure if she was pleasing her partner. Tess, and another friend of theirs, told Kris to treat a female partner the way she wanted to be treated.

All of Kris's senses were awakening. The smell of Tess was a mixture of lavender and honey. The sight of Tess's undergarments, silky and touching them was something that her own garments didn't do for her. Tess's soft whispers took Kris somewhere she had never been before. And her taste … the best way to describe it, honeydew.

What in the hell is wrong with me? Kris thought. *Why are THESE experiences filling my head?* It wasn't fair to Tony, but the thoughts would not go away. When Kris was with Tony, she was thinking of Tess. When Tony touched her, it wasn't Tony, it was Tess. When Tony kissed her, it wasn't Tony, it was Tess. Every image in her head was of Tess. It was Tess's smell and taste she was experiencing, and it was the soft moans of Tess she heard as they made love. As Tony and Kris were lying in each other's arms, she could feel Tess's arms wrapped around her waist, hearing her whisper into Kris's ear, telling her what an amazing lover she was.

Though Tony was a man's man. The smell of Coast soap, hopefully. Dirt under the fingernails. Rough hands, callused hands. His undergarments were not alluring. Grunts and moans. Nothing wrong with those qualities, but there was no preparation or thoughtfulness put into the display. The smells, the sounds, the feels, the tastes, the mannerisms, Tony could not compete with Tess, no man could.

Outside the bedroom, Tess was vibrant, loved being around her friends and talked about her family. She was a good mom, and her boys came first. Two of them were older and out of the house, but that did not matter to Tess. She was also very discreet about her and her husband's involvement in the lifestyle. Their children knew nothing about it, and they were careful to keep it that way.

Inside the bedroom, Tess was just as vibrant. She was also extremely sensual, compassionate and was an amazing lover. Tess was particularly good at helping Kris be comfortable. Physically, Tess was slightly shorter than Kris, had long, dark hair, a beautifully shaped body with curves in all of the right places. When Kris was with Tess, it wasn't just about the physical act of sex that made her a good lover. She was also incredibly good at the psychological and emotional aspect. Foreplay wasn't always about touching and kissing, but Kris did like to kiss her. Tess loved to laugh and have fun. They would talk and laugh as much as they would make love, and this was what put Kris at ease.

63

CHAPTER 15

Shaen's phone rang, and the screen read "unknown caller." "I thought we agreed to stop the calls for a while."

The voice on the other end of the line told Shaen the two needed to meet, that some developments had come up in the case with Kris.

"We don't need to meet. You need to let this all ride out until it is over. Her trial is going to be starting soon and we will be in the clear. Trust me, I have everything taken care of. I have from the start of all of this. Of course, none of this would have happened had Mack just left it all alone and not panicked. His threats of exposure set it all in motion. I promise, this will all be over with soon. Just sit tight, and don't panic like he did. No more contact until it's over. Kris will be in jail, and nobody will be any wiser to this."

Shaen had not panicked during this entire fiasco, until now. *What new development had taken place?* he wondered. He had to figure out what was going on without being caught snooping. He still knew one person he could call in the prosecutor's office, but it may not be helpful depending on which side the developments were on. He called anyway, just to see if they knew anything.

"Hey, it's Shaen. I have just heard there are some new developments in Kris's case. Anything I need to know?"

The male voice told him, "There isn't anything on our end. I have no clue what is happening other than what we already have, and you are aware of it. I honestly do not understand why you are so concerned with the progress of this case though. Is there something you need to tell me?"

"No. Mack was my partner, and she needs to pay for what she did. That is my interest in this." Shaen hoped that his statement was believable enough. He was sure that the multiple calls Mack made to him were known to Kris's attorney, but those were easily explained based on when they were made.

The man on the other end told Shaen, "I just hope we can get this case cleared with a guilty verdict. A lot of the evidence we have is circumstantial."

"How is that?" Shaen asked. "You have her nightstick which I am sure has her fingerprints."

"Just because her fingerprints are on them, doesn't make this solid evidence Shaen. Surely you understand that. Of COURSE, her prints are on it because it was her nightstick."

"You need to make sure the jury doesn't come up with any doubts as to whether or not Kris did this."

"Hey, Shaen, how about you let me do my job? I will say this—you are sounding like someone who has something to hide and want someone else to take the fall for it."

Shaen realized he went too far. "Like I said, Mack was my partner and I saw what was done to him. It makes me sick, and I want to make sure that bitch slowly rots in prison."

"I understand that, but you cannot call here asking questions, especially since you are on the witness list. It does not look good. Someone will be in contact with you about the day you are testifying."

"Fine," Shaen replied and abruptly hung up.

Richard McCullen hung up the phone with Shaen. This was the fifth call he had received from someone in the police department. Usually, it was Shaen. Ever since Mack was found, the focus of every investigation had been on Kris. Richard knew Kris had the motive. He was going to work the angle of revenge—revenge for the alleged rape which Richard was sure Mack had been guilty of. He heard rumors of other instances with Mack and female co-workers. The revenge angle would also work because Kris never received justice though the courts after attempting to file criminal charges.

There was nothing Richard could have done to file charges because of the statute of limitations. He was not sure if that was a good thing or not. Richard had received a lot of pressure from the department then too. Being the son of a captain, Mack was all but given free reign and could do just about anything without recourse. When Kris first went and spoke to detectives at the department, they immediately started pressuring Richard about tanking the case. It was a happy accident that the statute of limitations had run out. The flip side of that coin was that Mack would continue to go unpunished for the things he had done … that is, until he was found dead.

Adrienne contacted Ronnie to let her know she would be flying into St. Louis the Thursday before the trial. Ronnie asked for her flight information so she could pick her up and take her to Kris. "We are all coming in earlier that morning so this will be perfect. Trixie is coming to get me, so we can stick around the area until your flight comes in. Adrienne, you are more than welcome to stay with Trixie and me while you are here. There is no need to get a hotel room. We don't live far from Kris's parents' house either," Ronnie said.

"Thank you so much, Ronnie. I will take you up on that. How is your end of this going?"

"John, Penelope's investigator, and I have found quite a bit of information that will be immensely helpful to Kris's case. There are a couple of good leads we are tracking down."

"That is great news. Are you waiting to tell Kris?"

"Penelope wants to wait until we can sit down with Kris and tell her face to face. She wants some of this to be solid too."

"I can understand that" Adrienne said. "Well, I should let you go for now. I have to work on my notes from Kris's sessions and draft a report for the court before my testimony."

"Sounds good. I have some calls to make as well. I will see you next week," Ronnie said.

"I look forward to meeting you face to face Ronnie."

"The feeling is mutual, Adrienne."

It was just a little over a week before the trial, and Penelope was getting ready for her flight that coming Wednesday. Her phone rang, and it was her investigator, John Barker. "Hey John, what's happening?"

"Well, I was able to talk to some of the female officers Mack trained. Ronnie gave me their names, and I was able to get in contact with all three of them. Penny, they all three said Mack assaulted them at one point or another during the training, then followed them, harassed them, and threatened them to make sure they never said anything."

"That is fantastic!! Well, not fantastic that he did that, but fantastic that we can show a pattern of behavior. Do they still work for St. Louis?"

"One of them still works there, so she is not on board at this point as far as giving testimony. The other two live out of state but will do a deposition with their local courts and a court reporter if it will help you."

"It can't hurt. Prosecution may fight it, but we can always try. I will give their names and numbers to the circuit attorney's office so they can send someone or set something up with local courts. They may even be able to do a video conference deposition. Ronnie mentioned these ladies to me as well. I am glad you were able to contact them. Did they seem uneasy talking to you? I figured they would want to talk to Ronnie since they know her."

"Well, despite knowing her, they were uncomfortable talking to Ronnie because she is still on the department," John stated.

"I can understand that. Did you get anything else?" Penelope asked.

"Yes. Yes, I did. Elaine agreed to testify as well. She said she would dig up the notes from her sessions with Kris."

"Wait. I thought she told Kris she got rid of those notes a long time ago."

"She made copies and put them someplace safe when Mack started to threaten her. It was a good thing she did too, because she said someone had gone through her office during the same period, presumably looking for Kris's case notes."

"She must have been terrified when those calls started," Penelope said, partially thinking aloud.

"She was. She had already stopped her practice prior to being harassed but only recently, so she had not yet cleaned out her office. The very minute she got the first call from Mack, she made the copies to stash and shredded the original case file. This is how she was able to tell Kris she shredded the file and wasn't really lying. I also learned she bought a handgun to protect herself and her mom."

"As much as I hate to say this, every person who testifies for Kris with stories like Elaine's, will do nothing but help Kris. It is going to build a lot of doubt in the jurors' minds about Kris being the only person with a motive to kill Mack."

"Very true. I have some more good news if you want to hear it," John told her.

"This day is getting better and better," Penelope responded.

"Ronnie and I went to see the woman who Shaen arrested at the hotel during the prostitution sting. You know, the one he propositioned and assaulted promising to make her drug charges go away?"

"Yes, I know which one you are talking about. I really hope you are going to tell me she has agreed to testify."

"I am, but she said she would only do it on one condition. We need to provide her protection. She is absolutely terrified of Shaen and the reach he has."

"I will arrange for it, but it has to be done today because I will have to file her name with the courts with my other list of witnesses by tomorrow morning."

"Perfect. I will do that as soon as we hang up."

"Thank you, John. I appreciate all your arduous work."

"That is what you pay me for."

His senior year, Mack was no longer playing football. The hazing continued throughout the year and into the summer. It not only continued, but it escalated too. There was still name calling and women's items hanging from his locker, but one of his teammates went to the coach and told him Mack had tried to grope him in the showers after a practice. The boy didn't lie, and Mack could not take a chance of getting in trouble at home. One instance in the locker room led to another fight, which began with the downfall of Mack. He started getting into more fights and it got even more brutal each time he was caught looking at his teammates as they were changing clothes or showering, as well as getting caught by the others looking at the coach in a way that made THEM uncomfortable.

More than once, he went home with black eyes which were difficult to explain without getting in trouble at home, and now he had more disciplinary actions at school. On one occasion, Ms. Neylan gave him after school detention which would be served in her class. He sat down in a chair at the back of the room, slouched down and put his feet up on the chair in front of him.

Ms. Neylan walked into the room, sat on the edge of her desk, and stared at Mack. "Mr. Parkins, you need to sit up front, actually you need to be in the front row."

"Fine."

"Mack, I am not sure what has happened to you, but you are completely different than last year."

"I'm fine. Hey, I have a question for you."

"What is your question?"

"Why are you always staring at me in class? You did the same thing last year. That is what Debbie and I got into a fight about the day she threw my jersey at me. She caught me staring you." He sat down in the front row and looked at her. "Well?"

"I haven't been. That would be inappropriate."

"I think you want me." Mack had thought that everyone had wanted him for the last two years.

"Mr. Parkins, you are out of line."

"No, Ms. Neylan, YOU are out of line. I see you staring at me with a look on your face that

says you DO want me."

"You are mistaken."

"No."

She stood up and took a step closer to the desk Mack was sitting at. "I do not want you Mack, because I know that what you have been accused of being is true."

"Take it back." He snarled at her.

"I think I need to go get the principle."

Mack moved swiftly out of the desk chair and around to Ms. Neylan, grabbing her wrist. He was now bigger than she was thanks to his weightlifting the last two years. He grabbed her around her waist and pulled her to him, his other hand still around her wrist. "Admit it. You want me."

She stared at him, and lowered her voice, sheepishly saying, "Yes. I want you Mack, but you need to admit who you really are, at the very least to yourself."

His mind started racing and he thought about being in the locker room with his teammates.

He thought about when they were coming in and out of the showers. This is what got Mack excited enough to undo his pants and put Ms. Neylan's hand on him. As she began to rub him, he closed his eyes, threw his head back as she put her mouth on him. As he placed his hand on her head, the image of the football coach helped him finish. "Do you still think I am gay?".

She did not answer her, because the answer still would have been 'Yes'.

A few weeks after his detention, Mack began picking at the "weird" kids in the school. If they were smaller, smarter, or weak looking, Mack took his hazing out on them. He was angry for a lot of reasons, but the biggest was not being able to play ball. He just couldn't go back to being tormented, but he just couldn't quit either. Football was a very 'manly' thing to do in Texas. To not play football would be to take that manhood away. Over the summer, between his junior and senior year, Mack concocted a plan to make sure he never had to play ball again, and not because he quit.

One day while he was riding his bike to the restaurant, everyone still hung out at, he waited until a car was pulling away from the stop sign and purposefully let it hit him. When he went down, he whacked his head on the pavement, causing a pretty serious concussion. The doctor told his parents that one or two games would be okay, but not an entire season. The first serious hit could do permanent damage. This was the end of his football playing, so now, instead of people thinking he was 'a man' for playing football, they thought even MORE highly of him because he was able to endure so much pain from being hit by a car.

Debbie left the school about a week or so after Homecoming their junior year. Her parents moved to the other side of the state, allegedly because of her dad's job. 'Whatever,' he thought.

'I was done with her anyway.' He did not date anyone in his senior year either. He was trying too hard to keep from being suspended. The detentions were easier to explain.

About the only thing that saved him and allowed him to graduate, was the move from Texas half-way through his senior year. His father was offered a position with the St. Louis Police Department and since it was a higher position and better pay with benefits. The family was uprooted, and they moved to St. Louis.

CHAPTER 16

Another call was coming through to Penelope, so she ended the call with John.

"Hello, this is Penelope."

"Hey Penelope, it's Ronnie."

"Oh, hey. I did not look at the number when it rang through. What's going on Ronnie?"

"I have good news and bad news. Where would you like me to start?"

"Go ahead with the bad news first."

"Well, the mystery number is not going to be the case breaker, but the good news is, I found out who it belonged to." Ronnie said.

"Well…?" Penelope prodded.

"Mack gave the phone to a woman named Cathy. She originally worked at the area station house with everyone but went to the Record's Division. She would use the phone to give Mack information as to Kris's moves when she was in town trying to file the criminal charges. She knew the entire time what Kris was up to. She knew all of that, the attorney Kris originally went to see, everything."

"That explains the calls to Mack, but what about after he was found?"

"I went and spoke to her when I figured out who was using the number. On a hunch, I searched Shaen's records again because he is on the witness list for the prosecution.

Terry ran it down for me, but Shaen had one more call from that number. It turns out she and Shaen have been having an affair for quite some time now. She just used that phone since it was disposable, and if Shaen's wife ever saw the number pop up, he could say it was a work-related number."

"Do you think she may have told Shaen about the information she was passing to Mack?"

"No. She said Mack would pay her to give the information to him. Sometimes it was money and sometimes it was a gift. Shaen wasn't paying her."

"Sure, he was," Penelope responded. "He was paying her with sex."

Ronnie thought for a second. "This is true, but sex doesn't pay the bills and from what she said, Mack was paying her large sums of money for some of the information."

"I am still going to subpoena her. Anything I can do to create doubt, I am going to do."

"You may not need to subpoena her. She is pretty pissed off at Shane right now. She called to give him some information about our witness list, and he blew her off. He told her she would have to wait until this was all over before they could be in contact again. She felt like he was starting to play her."

"I will call her personally to see, but I will also have the subpoena filed just in case. She may change her feelings about him since they were seeing each other for so long before Mack was murdered. It surprises me that she wanted to give Shaen any information. She hadn't before this. WAIT! Do you think Mack knew about the affair and threatened to expose the two of them?"

"Why would he pay her then?"

"Maybe they were blackmailing each other?" Penelope asked. "This is getting so convoluted, but it's also looking better for Kris. What is Cathy like? Would she be capable of this?"

"Well, physically, she is strong. She worked out every day as far as I knew. She used to be heavy but lost a lot of weight. Personality wise— she had no problems stabbing someone in the back to get ahead. She is cunning, manipulative and can be downright mean. I can absolutely see her being capable of killing Mack, especially if he crossed her one too many times."

Ronnie continued, "I don't know why she decided to give Shaen information if she wasn't getting money from it. She just wanted to see him since he ghosted her since Mack had been found. I have been looking into his whereabouts in the time prior to Mack being found, the time with all the phone calls. Mack and Shaen don't talk for years, despite having been partners, and suddenly, Kris comes forward and there are almost daily calls between them right up until Mack is found."

"Do you think Shaen knew he was dead and just made the calls to make it look like he didn't know?"

"Penelope, I wouldn't put anything past Shaen at this point. Kris said Derrick described Shaen as being a 'follower' when he was in the department with Shaen. Derrick couldn't stand having to ride with Shaen because he was, and I quote, 'A complete pussy.'"

"Well, he developed a giant ego at some point. Based on what you and John have told me, he is arrogant and acts like he is perfect—a 'know it all.'"

"I am sure it is compensation for something else. Derrick said he was not confident at all. He either FOUND it or is over-doing it. Who knows? He could be good for Mack's murder too. I feel like Kris is already condemned because the deceased person was a police officer, and from what Terry told me, the people in the Homicide Division still are not looking any further than Kris. As far as that department is concerned, Kris killed Mack and they will make sure she pays for it."

Penelope told her she would have John look into Shaen even more than what they have been. "In the meantime, talk to Kris. Give her something in the way of information to keep her spirits up if you want. I will call her later too."

When they hung up, Penelope made the arrangements and texted John to take the woman from the hotel incident to a safe place. She filed her name with the courts as well as adding Cathy to the witness list for the defense. She had left her office and was driving home when her phone rang.

Richard knew he did not have a solid case. He had circumstantial evidence and a lot of speculation. There were so many other people that had a motive to kill Mack, and he was doing what he could. He picked up the phone and called Kris's attorney.

"Ms. Clinton, this is Richard McCullen. I am calling to see if Mrs. Parker would like to make a plea deal. We can meet after she arrives in town next week."

"The answer is 'no' counselor. It is not going to happen."

"Really? You haven't even heard what I am offering, and unless she is sitting right there with you, she doesn't know you are answering for her without discussing it."

"I will tell you what Mr. McCullen, I will get her on the line right now. Hold please." Before Richard could respond, Penelope put the call on hold and dialed Kris. She picked up the phone on the first ring.

"Penelope, do you have anything new?" Kris asked.

"Kris, I am going to merge a call into this one before we discuss anything else. The prosecutor wants to know if you want to take a plea deal. I already told him 'No,' but he wants to hear it from you."

"Okay," Kris replied.

"Mr. McCullen, Kris is on the line. I am not recording this call. Please tell Mrs. Parker your offer."

"Mrs. Parker, my office is willing to offer 25 years without parole."

Penelope spoke up. "Kris, what do you want to do? I will follow your decision."

Kris paused because she was doing her best to keep from laughing aloud at the absurdity of it all. "Mr. McCullen, with all due respect sir, you can shove that offer up your ass. THAT is how sure I am that I did NOT do this or play any part in the death of Mack Parkins. I will take my chances with a jury."

"There you have it Mr. McCullen. You should have taken my 'no.' At least I was nicer about it. Thanks for your time. Kris, I will call you right back as soon as all these connections are gone. I wouldn't want anyone hearing what we discuss and claiming they didn't realize the phone wasn't hung up."

'Well, that didn't go as well as I hoped, but it did go exactly as I thought it would', Richard thought to himself.

Kris's phone rang again. "Yes ma'am?" Kris said to Penelope.

"You had me a little worried when you paused before answering him."

"Penelope, I was trying hard to keep from laughing. What an ass! He should have just said 'We are offering you a life sentence.' Even I knew the only reason he offered a deal is because everything they have is circumstantial. Yes, my fingerprints are on the nightstick, but it is my nightstick. Do they think I am stupid?"

"There she is! The fighter I know you are, and they must think so. They must have forgotten you were in police work and how the courts work too. You are correct, other than the fingerprints on something that belongs to you, it is circumstantial at best. Please do not forget that people have been found guilty in cases like this but let me reassure you that we have enough to plant doubt in the jury's mind if they already think you are the only one to have had motive."

"That is good to know. So, I am guessing you have found more avenues to take this case?"

"Yes, ma'am we have. Ronnie and John have been working around the clock tracking down leads. Ronnie was going to call you and let you know, but I will tell you a little bit.

CHAPTER 17

Richard picked up the phone again, this time calling the supervisor of the homicide division.

"Hey, this is Richard. She declined the deal."

"I would figure she would have jumped at that offer. She surely would have saved herself the ordeal of a trial. What are you doing to make sure she is convicted?"

"Captain, you do understand that I cannot 'make sure' of anything right? You have been around the courts long enough to know that. I will present the evidence I have, and it is up to the jury after that."

"Surely there is something you can do to bolster the efficacy of the evidence. That woman killed one of our own and she needs to pay for this Richard."

"Again, all I can do is present the evidence. I will not embellish anything. I will not fabricate evidence or do anything to what evidence I may have already. Maybe YOUR detectives should have done a better job at their investigations. Do not forget Captain, Kris was also 'one of your own,' or do you only protect the ones you deem worthy of your protection?"

"You better check yourself, Richard. My detectives did their due diligence in their investigation, and you need to do yours with the courts."

This was the second time today Richard's face turned purple in color from anger. "Captain, that sounded oddly like a threat, veiled or not, you are speaking to an officer of the courts, and I can and WILL have you charged."

"Look Richard, we just want her convicted. She falsely accused Mack of rape and then when she didn't get her way in seeing that he went to jail, she killed him."

"I can assure you; her accusations were not false. Mack got lucky on a technicality. I have had more victims besides Kris who were victimized by Mack. Some of them missed out on justice because of the statutes and some because he died. At least I had more than circumstantial evidence in those cases."

"HAD being the operative word," the captain said.

"Richard could hear gratification in the captain's voice. "Another case that had evidence issues. Funny how the evidence went in favor of Mack that go-around. One of these days, this is going to bite you ALL in the ass. The cover-ups have got to stop at some point. The department may be paying my boss a lot of money, but you better damn well hope I am never put in charge."

The captain laughed, "And yet here you are 'Dick,' keeping your mouth shut to save your job. You are a 'Yes Man' just like everyone else."

"Just because I haven't done anything, doesn't mean I don't want to. I will say it a million times…the police department got INCREDIBLY lucky with the statute of limitations."

"Richard, we better have a little more luck with a conviction of Kris Parker. What she did to Mack is absolutely disgusting."

"Based on what I have read about the rape, and everything I personally know of him; he fucking deserved it." With that, Richard slammed down the phone.

One of Richard's co-workers, Ingrid Harris, passed by the door. "Richard, are you okay?"

"No but thank you for asking."

"Is there anything I can do?"

"Only if you can figure out a way to make sure the right people go to jail. That fucking police department has a serious problem."

"You got the Parker case, didn't you?"

"I did. It makes me sick to have to work on this case at all. I know what the mother fucker did to her. She should get a medal not be in a courtroom. I bet you are sorry you asked."

"No, I'm not. I really wish there was something I could do," Ingrid said. "I know you are in the same boat I am," Richard told her.

"At least I am newer here. Chief doesn't trust me yet."

"If you can get out of this job early, I will help you find someplace else to work. Once it gears up, you won't get out. It's like making a deal with the devil. You will pick the wrong direction at The Crossroads if you aren't careful."

Ingrid could see tears welling up in his eyes. '*What the hell did I get myself into?*' she asked herself. Richard was sitting in his office gazing at the walls. He was in a serious bind and had to do something. He had about a week left before the trial, he was getting a horrible amount of backlash over this case, pressure from his boss, the Board of Police Commissioners, nearly every member of the homicide squad and 95 percent of the rest of the department, including some of the women. This case is going to be a local media circus and he was forced to become the ringmaster. The spotlights all focused on him. It was at that very moment that Richard knew exactly what he needed to do.

CHAPTER 18

Penelope proceeded to tell Kris about Mack's additional victims but left out the woman from the hotel who had been victimized by Shaen. Kris was in tears because there seemed to be just a glimmer of hope for her. "So, are they going to testify as character witnesses?"

"I am going to subpoena them, but the only way I can put them on the stand is if the prosecution brings up your rape, which he undoubtably will because it is the biggest motive for you allegedly killing Mack. These other victims will help place doubt because they, too, have motive. Does this all make sense? I know you are familiar with court procedure but from a different angle. I am not trying to sound condescending."

"Oh, I didn't feel like that at all, and yes, it makes complete sense," Kris replied.

"Good. Please do not hesitate if you have any questions between now and next Wednesday."

"I should be okay. Who all will be on the flight with us?"

"It will be me, Ronnie, and Terry. Terry is there for an official police escort. Is Tony still going on the flight?"

"Yes, he will be there."

"Perfect. Okay, Kris, I will see you on Wednesday evening. Take a deep breath, Hunnie, it is all going to be okay."

"Thank you, Penelope."

They disconnected the call, and Penelope finished some last-minute things on her list before packing what she needed. Kris was getting dinner ready when Tony walked in from work. The puppies greeted him at the door and were still dancing around his feet when he walked into the kitchen. The oldest, Beau, jumped onto a kitchen chair and leapt into Tony's arms.

"How was work?" Kris asked.

"Not too bad. I took tomorrow off so I could help you get ready, and we can start packing."

"Thank you. I really appreciate that. I talked to Penelope today. They found some of Mack's other victims." She explained what Penelope told her. Tony did not say anything and just hugged Kris. She still felt so safe in his tight embrace, despite the tension that was between them, especially when they were being intimate, on the exceedingly rare occasions they were. She and Tony had not been a part of the swinger's community for quite some time, but from time to time, Kris could not help but miss those intimate moments with Tess. Kris did not understand why she craved Tess's touch more than she did Tony's.

Tony broke the embrace, kissed her on the top of her head and said, "Let me get out of these work clothes, and I will help with the rest of dinner."

"Okay. Take your time."

When they finished eating, they sat outside at the fire pit and had a glass of wine. The dogs were running around, chasing each other. The female, Belle, jumped into Kris's lap and began licking her face. Kris started to cry, praying this was not the last time she was able to experience this part of life.

The following Wednesday morning was spent with everyone preparing for flights. Tony and Kris had the house/dog sitter lined up. Penelope had some notes to work on, and Ronnie was making last minute calls with John. Terry was planning with the local police department to make sure they did not get stopped at the airport. Early in the evening, Tony picked everyone up at the airport. When they arrived at the house, Tony ordered food for delivery. Kris's case was not discussed until after dinner, and Terry had been taken to the hotel. Ronnie asked Kris, "How are you feeling K.C.?"

"I am doing okay Ronnie. I am going through phases of difficulties, but I am feeling a little better. Is it too much to ask or even wish for the person who killed Mack to come forward?"

"From your lips to God's ears Kris," Ronnie replied. "John and I have some pretty solid information that will help your case, but no such luck on the mystery person coming forward."

"Of course not. This is me we are talking about."

"I still have hope that this is all going to play out in the right direction, K.C."

"What about Shaen? Where is he in all of this?" Kris asked.

"Oh, we have paths we are following with him too. I have got you woman. I have told you many times in the past and I am telling you now, I've got your six. This is all going to be okay."

Penelope walked back into the room, and they began to discuss strategy. The conversation wasn't too in-depth because the flight was early, and everyone needed sleep. Kris's parents were meeting them at the airport so they could take Kris home. All three dogs joined Tony and Kris in bed. Then came the kitties. It was a wonder they were able to get any sleep at all. Kris felt a lot of comfort having them all there. She was still on the fence as to whether she would see them again. There was truly little room in the bed, but she didn't care. She was content and more relaxed than she had been in a long time.

The morning seemed to come earlier than expected. Kris was awakened by wagging tails and kisses from all the four-legged babies. They sensed her nervousness and fear, cuddling with her all night long. Kris could not help but cry all morning as she was getting ready to leave. '*This may very well be the last time I get to be here*', she thought. Everyone was silent on the way to the airport. Kris loved on the babies, telling them she had to go to work and would be home soon. That was her hope at least. The tears continued to flow, and there was no stopping them. Tony and Ronnie both did their best to comfort Kris, but the only thing that would help at this point truly was for the person who killed Mack to either come forward or be found before the judge's gavel came down one last time, or for it to fall in Kris's favor.

The flight to St. Louis lasted for what seemed like an eternity. Kris's parents were at the airport, waiting as they all came out of the gates. She held on to her mom and dad for a long time, sobbing and shaking. As she finally broke their embrace, she looked across the terminal, seeing a man she thought she recognized. He was clearly paying attention to Kris and all the things happening with her. He looked to be between 5'8" and 5'10", but it was hard to tell due to the distance. She could tell that the man was already going bald because of the receding hair line and the close "buzz' cut. Still, there was something awfully familiar about him. He walked like he had a stick in his ass that he was trying to keep from falling out. There was a cockiness to him, and it was the cockiness that was giving off the familiarity.

Kris finally wrote off the man as being airport security. That would explain why he was paying such close attention to them. Even though Kris was not handcuffed, it was obvious police officers were escorting her. All she wanted at this moment was to be on a return flight back to Virginia with Tony.

CHAPTER 19

Richard woke early on Thursday. He had less than a week before the start of the trial. He needed to start his opening statement. Normally, he would have already had this done, but he had not been up to doing it this time. His co-chair, Ingrid, was one of the best young attorneys he had ever seen. She had a way with words and could outwit anyone. Richard was quite a bit older than Ingrid, so her personality and her intelligence reminded him of his daughter. She too, was bright and happy. She was intelligent and she was going places in her career. His mind drifted for a moment, and he turned back to the task at hand.

Derrick knew something about the case that neither Kris nor anyone else knew for that matter. He had a conversation with Richard not long before Kris got back in town and was going to hear from him again before the end of the trial. Richard had been very aloof, but Derrick wanted to hear what he had to say, especially if it was something that would benefit Kris. He was married and had four children, but Derrick always loved Kris, and always would. When Kris told him about what happened to her, he was absolutely beside himself. He fought the urge to hunt Shaen and Mack both down and do to them what they did to her, or at the very least, beat them both to a bloody mess. Derrick knew this would not have done Kris any good. It was clear that she would have taken the blame for that too. *What a bunch of assholes in that place.* Derrick thought. *They wanted to hang Kris out to dry when she was still a cop, and they are still trying it.*

He wondered if the rape being orchestrated by Mack was what they did to get Kris to leave the department. The worse part, aside from the obvious, was knowing Kris had no choice in anything. She should have been able to make the decision to leave the department all on her own. They took that away from her in one moment. He could not get over his own hurt for her. She left her job because she was miserable and did not even know why she was. They never gave her a chance, and in all reality, could have killed her with the amount of whatever they gave her to render her helpless. Derrick knew the mind set of them both and thank God it did not kill Kris. Mack and Shaen, especially Mack, were both cold enough to have dumped her and left her all alone.

The more scenarios he thought of that COULD have happened, the more upset Derrick became. The tears started to well up in his eyes when his phone rang, "Special Agent Hinton. How may I help you?"

Richard stopped in the middle of writing, picked up the phone and dialed it. "Special Agent Hinton, this is Richard McCullen. Is this a good time to talk?"

"Yes, but I am going to call you back from a secure line. These are recorded at all times." Derrick got a number to call Richard back, stepped outside his building and went to his car to sit. He called Richard back. "Okay, now we are good to go."

Richard started filling Derrick in on his plans and explained to Derrick what he would need from him. "Are you able to do all of this?" Richard asked.

"Absolutely Mr. McCullen. I have to say, I am a little floored, but glad to hear this is the way you decided to proceed. I will make sure everything is in place when you are ready."

"Does that include for my co-chair?" Richard asked.

"Yes, Sir. It will all be taken care of."

"I will be sure to call you the day before it all happens, that way you can get everyone together that you need. This is going to be a crazy situation, so if you need extra time to get people together, I can stall a couple of things."

"That shouldn't be a problem. You let me know if you need anything else from me."

"I will. Thank you, Special Agent."

"Please, call me Derrick in this arena. No need to be so formal. In the meantime, I will see you very soon. I came into the office today to wrap things up before a red-eye flight."

"Sounds good Derrick. See you soon."

Both men hung up the phone. Derrick leaned his head back, tears rolling down his cheeks. '*Well, holy shit*', he thought to himself. '*This is really happening.*'

The call ended and Richard felt a million times better. He knew he was doing the right thing. He went back to writing his opening statement. The words flowed much easier this time. *Yes,* he thought. '*This is the right choice.*'

CHAPTER 20

When Kris and everyone else got to her parent's house, Penelope and Kris checked in with the courts so they knew Kris made it into town. She was not allowed to go anywhere except to be taken to and from the trial. She and Tony settled in at her parents' house after all of the "business" was out of the way. Penelope told Kris her phone would be on and to call day or night if she needed it. Ronnie went back home but told Kris she would be over the following day. She said she had something to bring her that she may need before and during the trial. "A lock pick and a nail file for an escape?" Kris laughingly asked.

"Funny, but not funny K.C. Don't get me wrong, I am glad you are still able to be a smart ass, but …" Ronnie started to say.

"I know, I know. I have to do something, or I will go crazy."

"I know you do. It is all going to be okay."

Kris couldn't help but feel a little resigned at this point, "That is what everyone keeps telling me."

On that Friday morning, Kris got up, took a shower, and sat talking with her parents. After a while, Tony and her dad went to the store and picked up some groceries and brought home some lunch. After lunch, Kat and Lilly showed up, again, everyone talking about anything EXCEPT what was going on. Kris was exhausted. "I am going to go lay down for a while. I am starting to get a headache I am so mentally drained," she told everyone.

"Do you want me to come lay down with you?" Tony asked. "I will be okay but feel free if you want to," she told him.

"I may be in there in a bit." He kissed her and wrapped his arms around her tightly. For a brief moment, she felt completely at ease and as though nothing was wrong.

Kris knew he was worried about her, but she reassured him she would not do anything stupid. She was still asleep when Ronnie arrived at the house with Adrienne. Adrienne, Ronnie, Tony, and Kris's family were all at the house at this point and were in the kitchen, quietly talking so they wouldn't wake Kris. Tony was the first one to hear Kris crying from the back bedroom where she was sleeping. As he started to get up and go to her, Adrienne said, "Do you want me to take this one Tony?"

"Do you mind? I think she is having a nightmare. Be careful though, because when she is deep in it, she wakes up swinging."

"Thanks for the warning, and I don't mind at all. Is that okay with you Mrs. Clarke?" Adrienne said turning to Kris's mom.

"That would be fine, Adrienne. You probably know how to handle it better than the rest of us."

"Which room is she in?"

Tony directed Adrienne to the last room on the right, and as she approached the end of the hall, could hear Kris crying and calling out. Tony was right, it was a nightmare. She quietly opened the door and approached the bed. Kris was lying with her back to the door and a pillow pulled up to her chest, griping it tightly. On her right ankle was a black, bulky monitor that had been placed on Kris back in Virginia. She sat on the edge of the bed, very lightly putting her hand on Kris's shoulder. She addressed Kris quietly and the moment Adrienne said her name, she knew it was a mistake. Kris must have been in a very intense part of the nightmare because just as Tony predicted, Kris whipped around, left fist swinging. Adrienne was far enough away that she was able to stop Kris's flying arm and fist. She said a little louder, "Kris, it's okay. It's Adrienne. You are okay, and you are safe. You are at your parent's house. Sweetie, wake up."

Kris was shaking as she woke, still disoriented and staring at Adrienne until she finally realized where she was. She could not figure out why Adrienne was there. "What the hell? What is happening?"

"I am going to be testifying, remember?" Adrienne reminded Kris.

"Yes. I remember, but why are you here so early?"

"Because you have a lot of people who love you and are worried about you. Tell me what that was all about." She said referring to the nightmare.

It finally dawned on Kris that she woke up swinging. "OH MY GOD!!! Adrienne, I am so sorry. I swung at you. Did I hit you?"

"No, you didn't hit me. I am sorry for startling you."

"It's okay. I will be fine."

"You are shaking sweetie. What was this one about?" Of course, as her therapist, Adrienne was well aware of the nightmares.

"Much of the same as they always are. This time it came with the added bonus of being hauled off to prison."

"Oh, Kris. You are not going to go to prison."

"Again, everyone keeps telling me that, but I am still not believing it. I have visions of being in a cell with a very large woman named 'Big Bertha' and she is going to make me her 'bitch.'"

Adrienne could not help but laugh. "I'm sorry, but the way you said that is cracking me up."

Kris couldn't help but laugh at that point. "Sometimes I really don't like you, Adrienne," Kris said to her with a smile on her face.

"I know, but you love me," Adrienne replied.

"Fuck you, Adrienne," Kris replied laughing.

"Aw, fuck you too Kris," Adrienne said as she rubbed her hand across Kris's shoulders in a comforting way. "Do you need more sleep?"

"Yes, but I am afraid to go to sleep. I am afraid the nightmares will start again. I don't want to be alone."

"Hang on, and I will go get Tony."

"Honestly, Adriene, as much as he tries, he isn't much help. Everything is so tense with us right now. His constant affairs are triggering me, and I don't even want to sleep in the same bed as him."

"I can sit here with you, or I can have your mom come back. Which do you prefer?"

"Would you mind doing some EMDR work with me to see if that will help me relax a little more?" Kris asked her.

"Not at all. That is a great idea."

Kris and Adrienne did some EMDR work. Kris becoming more relaxed; her mind working the negative images from the nightmare out for the moment. Adrienne's voice was very soothing and as they talked through everything, Adrienne stopped with the EMDR, and they just started to chat. Nothing was brought up about the trial starting on Monday, the stressors in Kris and Tony's marriage, or family stress which had also been plaguing Kris. They talked and laughed like two old friends. As Kris began to fall asleep, Adrienne started to stand up. Kris could feel the pressure releasing off of the bed. "Please don't go just yet. Will you wait until I really fall asleep?"

"I can do that." Adrienne grabbed a couple of pillows from the floor and leaned against the headboard of the bed. Kris turned over, lying on her left side, so her back was to Adrienne. As Kris started to fall asleep, Adrienne felt her jerk a couple of times, whimpering like she was starting to cry. Adrienne leaned down closer to Kris's ear and whispered to her, "It's okay, Kris. You are safe at home and surrounded by people who love you. We aren't going to let anything happen to you. Adrienne began rubbing Kris's shoulder. "I promise you; you are safe. Nothing is going to happen to you. This is all going to be okay."

Adrienne could feel Kris's body start to relax. Her shoulder dropped as Adrienne continued to talk to her, "Remember, your bed is a cloud, soft, but strong enough to keep you falling through. Let it surround you, keep you safe and warm. Let your body sink into the cloud, clear your mind of the things that do not serve you well." Adrienne was pretty tired herself. Her flight had left just after Kris's and that was an early flight as well. She got leaning against the headboard, on top of the covers next to Kris as she, too, drifted off to sleep.

CHAPTER 21

Ronnie was in the kitchen with Tony, Kris's parents, and Kris's sisters. "I am going to go back and see if they want us to fire up the grill." Ronnie walked down the hall to the bedroom, slowly opened the door and was about to ask Kris and Adrienne about dinner, when she saw Adrienne sleeping in a seated position behind Kris, her hand on Kris's shoulder, but lying on top of the covers. Ronnie gently laid a blanket across Adrienne and quietly left the room. When she returned to the kitchen, Kris's mom asked if they should start cooking. "I wouldn't just yet Mrs. Clarke. Adrienne managed to get K.C. back to sleep and will stay there to make sure she can get some good rest. Let's give it an hour, and then I will tell them we are starting dinner." Ronnie did not mention to anyone that Kris and Adrienne were BOTH asleep on the small bed together.   It was a scene that confirmed the suspicion Ronnie had of Kris for a long time. Ronnie was sure that Kris was not aware of who she really was. Kris had confided in Ronnie about her and Tony's involvement in the swinger's group, as well as Kris's physical relationship with Tess. When Kris talked about Tess, there was something different in her voice, but it wasn't something that even Kris recognized. Ronnie knew what it was because she had been there once too. *She will figure it out*, Ronnie thought.

Kris opened her eyes and lay in bed, thinking about what was to come on Monday. She could feel the ankle monitor weighing on her, and tears started falling from her eyes. She was aware of Adrienne's presence next to her, and as Kris started to gently slide from the bed, she felt Adrienne's hand slightly tighten on her arm. "Are you okay Kris?"

"I'm good. I was just getting up to grab something." Kris's back was still to Adrienne, so she was sure it wasn't obvious she was crying. She was wrong and knew it when Adrienne produced some tissues from the nightstand. "Good Lord woman, do you have tissues in a 'Mary Poppins' bag?"

Adrienne couldn't help but laugh, "No, smart ass, I don't. There are some on this side of the bed. Did you have another nightmare?"

"No. I'm just scared. It's the unknown of all of this. I did not do this, and I am terrified beyond words that I am going to be in prison for the rest of my life," Kris said through the falling tears.

"Kris, we all know you did not kill Mack. Penelope is a smart cookie, and we all have faith that she will not let you go to prison for something you did not do. You need to have that same faith."

"I'm trying Adrienne, I really am. I am trying really hard to stress only about this trial, but it is difficult knowing that Tony is cheating again. If ever there was a time that I REALLY needed to trust him and have him comfort me, it is now and that just isn't possible."

"Can I ask you a question?"

Kris laughed a little at her question. "Isn't that what you get paid to do?"

"Good point. Are you still in love with Tony?"

"I love him very much."

"That is not what I asked you Kris, but good try."

"Honestly, I don't think I am. As much as I want him to hold me, and to be intimate with me, I am not comfortable with him. Does that make sense?"

Adrienne smiled, "It makes perfect sense. I see the connection between the two of you. The friendship aspect is so strong, and I know you love him and care about him. Is there someone else you are in love with?"

"No," Kris answered quickly.

"Is there someone else you are more comfortable with in a physical sense? I know you are no longer part of the swinger's community, but I know you are still friends with people from the group. Are you still involved with someone?"

"No, I am not cheating on Tony."

"I didn't say you were sweetie, but I get the sense that you are emotionally attached to someone from that group of friends."

"I honestly haven't considered it. I still enjoy hanging out with Tess and a few others, but that is about it." As she was telling Adrienne she could not help but to let memories of her and Tess together, as well as dreams she had had about Adrienne creep into her head. The latter memory is not something she disclosed to Adrienne, nor would she ever.

"Are you comfortable with Tess? Would you like me to call and see if she can come for the trial? As you know, I am here for you, but any interactions have to be 'business' in the courtroom. Does that make sense?"

"Yes, of course it does, and yes, you can call her if you want."

"I will do that after dinner. Do you think you could eat yet?"

"Yeah. I am hungry, and I can smell the food from the kitchen. I am pretty sure Mom is making her potato salad. I can smell the dill."

Adrienne stood up from the bed, walked to the other side and knelt down in front of Kris, who was sitting on the edge. She took Kris's face in both hands and stared directly into her eyes. Kris could feel an electricity that she had only ever felt with Tess. It was difficult for Kris to keep eye contact at this point. "Kris, this WILL be okay. You are NOT going to prison."

Tears started again, partially because of the fear Kris was feeling about the trial and partially because of what she was feeling in general about where her mind had been wandering off to, especially in instances just like this. The fact that when she and Tony were intimately involved, she could only think of her and Tess, and now, being this close to Adrienne, she was feeling things she had never felt. It felt like a betrayal—a betrayal to Tony, to their marriage vows and to herself. The worst part of it all, somehow Kris's family had become aware of Kris and Tony's involvement in the swinger's community. At first her parents did not believe the information, but one day, during an argument on the phone with her mom, she became so frustrated that she emailed everyone in her family and told them everything that had happened between her and Tony. Neither Kris nor Tony knew who said something, but Kris's parents were absolutely disgusted. They could not understand how she could be a part of "something like that." This was one of the times, and there were many over the years, that Kris heard her mother say, "You were not raised that way." After that came the blame being heaped on Kris. Her mom told Kris it was basically her fault that Tony was cheating, and it would never have happened had they not become involved with the swinger's community. Her mom believed that Kris opened the door to cheating when another person was brought into the marriage. Cat and Lilly looked at her differently too. They treated her like she was a criminal, looking at her like she had the plague.

Now, sitting there, Adrienne mere inches from her face, Kris found herself wondering how they would all react to Kris feeling the way she does when in an intimate situation with a woman. Hell, Kris didn't even know how to react. She couldn't figure out why she was feeling the way she was. "Kris, are you still with me?" She heard Adrienne ask.

"Yes, sorry. I was just thinking about something."

"Want to share?"

"Yes and no. No because it is slightly embarrassing and yes, only because you will eventually drag it out of me."

"Would you rather wait until later, after dinner?"

"That would be fine," Kris told her. Their gaze had not broken, but now Adrienne's hands were on Kris's knees.

"You know how we end a session right?" Adrienne asked.

"Biggest hug ever," Kris responded.

As they stood and hugged, Kris felt herself relaxing more than she had in a long time. Adrienne got close to Kris's ear and said, "You don't have to tell me what is so embarrassing. I already know. In time you can, but not now."

Kris looked at her quizzically. "I know what you are feeling, and we can work through those feelings, but not now, not here. There are more pressing matters to attend to, okay?"

"Yes," Kris said.

"Let's go eat," Adrienne said, kissing Kris on the cheek.

CHAPTER 22

The rest of the evening went fairly well. Tony was being very attentive to Kris. There was still tension between them. Kris was sure everyone else could sense it too. The air felt heavy and there were so many elephants in the room. The trial was only a couple of days away, and while Kris's parents were being supportive, they were also swallowing a lot of what they really wanted to say. Even Ronnie was looking at Kris oddly. She couldn't quite figure out why, but Ronnie kept glancing at Kris and Adrienne. Ronnie knew about Tony and Kris's activities, but she would never have said a thing to anyone in Kris's family. Of course, Katie knew too, but Kris had no worries about her either. Neither of them was judgmental about it, and understood why Kris got involved but did not understand the "lifestyle" as a whole. The biggest aspect that was hard for anyone to understand was how it was so easy for one spouse to allow another man or woman to be intimate with their partner.

The dynamics of those relationships were different for everyone. Some couples would "swap" partners, go into different rooms; some would be in the same room and others would bring a single person to join that couple. Most of the time Kris didn't understand it either. All she knew at that time was she was trying to keep her marriage together. The idea of being part of this was brought up long before she and Tony got involved. When they were first married and living in San Diego, Tony talked about going to a swinger's club in the area. Kris toyed with the idea, but it never came to fruition. Kris couldn't bring herself to it because she knew she was a jealous person and the thought of seeing or knowing Tony was with another woman was too much for her.

It wasn't until years later that Kris gave in and Tony brought a woman he worked with home for them to open the door to these experiences. It had been Kris's first experience with a woman, and it was not the best, so it was a long time before she would agree to that again. When she did, it was after they were already involved in the community, and it was also the beginning of Tony's cheating—at least as far as Kris knew. The first woman Tony cheated with was someone they would occasionally play with, but Kris thought it was safe, because the woman was also married and lived a few hours away. When the woman started to visit more frequently, she started staying at the house more and more. Kris likened the entire experience to inviting a vampire into your home because once you invite them in, they don't have to leave. This was the case for quite some time. When the cheating started, there was no amount of explaining Kris could do to her parents that she really felt like what she was doing was what was best for the marriage. At the time, Tony was very happy and in Kris's head, it was the most important thing she could do.

That night, Kris couldn't eat much. Her stomach was in knots, and she only had a short time before the start of the trial. She spent more time moving food around her plate than eating it. The conversations were as strained as the moods. Everyone jumped when Adrienne's phone rang. For some reason, Kris burst into laughter. "Well, that woke us all up in a hurry." She couldn't stop laughing. Adrienne excused herself, laughing with everyone else. Kris overheard Adrienne say, "Oh! That is absolutely wonderful. Kris will be happy to know that. Okay, someone will meet you at the airport. Safe travels."

When she walked back into the room, Kris's mom asked, "What was that about if you don't mind my asking?"

"Not at all. Kris, your friend Tess is flying in tomorrow morning. Tony, will you pick her up since she knows you?"

"Of course, I will."

"She is going to text me the information so I will just forward it to you."

"That will work for me."

Kris's mom looked like she was sorry she asked. She was sure Tess was one of the people involved in the group Tony and Kris were in, but she wasn't sure how or to what extent. Right now, she could only worry about what was going to happen with Kris at this trial. What she really hoped was that nobody else knew about Kris and Tony's activities. She didn't raise her daughter to become involved with something so "deviant" as that. It had to have been Tony's idea to begin with and neither she nor Kris's father were happy about it. *What could she have been thinking?* When Kris told them the details of what had been going on in the marriage, her mom told her, "This was not something any of us needed to know."

Despite all of this and not being happy with a lot of the choices in Kris's life, Kris's parents were not going to abandon her during this difficult time. They posted the bail, which they were sure they would get back because they knew, as her parents and the people who raised her, their daughter would not have killed Mack. EVERYONE knew she had enough motive to do it, but deep down, there was no way Kris would have killed him.

Kris was feeling even more tension than before. She was thrilled that everyone was coming to support her. Her and Tony's former neighbor was coming in from West Virginia as well as friends from Virginia, and of course everyone she knew in the St. Louis area. With Tess coming and knowing that her family knew exactly who she was, Kris was becoming increasingly stressed out. The distance that this information coming out had caused between Kris and her family truly hurt Kris to the core. This hurt led to anger and resentment toward Tony, which always led to more arguing. To top it all off, as she had mentioned to Adrienne, she was sure that Tony was cheating again. *I just don't have the time or the energy for his crap right now. I need to focus on me,* Kris thought. *It will have to wait until after this is over. Then again, is it REALLY bothering me? I love him, but it's different now.*

She would eventually bring this up to Adrienne in greater length, and they touched on it a little while ago, but it was more about how Kris was feeling because of the previous affairs. There were a LOT of things they needed to discuss when this was all over. It was getting late as they all sat around the table chatting. "I am getting tired again," Kris announced. "I think I am going to go ahead and go to bed."

"I'm not too far behind you," Tony told her.

"Mom, do you want some help cleaning up the kitchen? I never realized how messy my friends are," she said laughing.

Ronnie launched a wadded-up napkin at Kris as she stood up, "Go to bed Sleeping Beauty. Your messy friends will take care of the clean-up." Ronnie came to the other side of the table. "Get some sleep K.C." she said as she hugged Kris. "We will see you tomorrow."

Kris hugged and said good night to everyone. She hugged her parents last and held on tight to her mom and dad both, taking in the comfort of their embrace. Her mom put her hands on either side of Kris's face, looked into her eyes and said, "This is going to be okay, Baby Girl. You are going to be okay." Kris's mom had always had a coolness in her hands that was very comforting. When Kris was little, and really sick, her mom's hands always made her feel better, just as they were doing right now. It was comforting, and for the first time, Kris was starting to think that everything really was going to be okay.

"I love you, Momma."

"I love you too Baby Girl. Get some sleep."

CHAPTER 23

Kris went back into the bedroom, and laid down, snuggled under the covers. She listened to the background noise of the conversations and light laughter coming from the kitchen. *They must not be too worried, or nobody would be laughing,* Kris thought. She drifted off to sleep and felt Tony get into the bed beside her, his arm drawing her to his chest, holding her tight. Despite all of the issues they were having, and Kris not feeling comfortable with Tony in a more intimate capacity, she still felt very safe in his arms. For now, they were both able to pretend there weren't any issues in their marriage.

The following day, Tony went to the airport and picked up Tess. Adrienne secured a room for her at a hotel, which was just across the highway from where Kris grew up. After Tess was settled into her room, she and Adrienne drove back over to Kris's parents' house, Ronnie came back with Trixie. Katie and her husband came over, as well as Annie and Lynn, childhood school friends that are more like non-blood sisters. It was so comforting to have all her friends around her, even if it was for the trial. The love and support were quite evident and helped put Kris in a better frame of mind. Penelope was planning to come over later in the day so she and Kris could go over some last-minute items pertaining to the trial. The evening was fairly relaxing again, with Kris surrounded by family and friends. Of course, the trial looming in the very near future was still causing some stress. Adrienne pulled Kris aside before dinner so they could do some EMDR work which helped Kris tremendously.

Penelope arrived with files in hand. She, Kris, and Ronnie sat at a table in the basement where they had some privacy. Penelope handed Kris the list of questions she was going to ask,   "I want to go over these with you and give you an idea of what I think the prosecutor will ask on cross- examination. Are you ready?"

"As ready as I will ever be," Kris replied.

Ronnie read the questions as Penelope countered with the "prosecution" side of things. A few times Kris had become increasingly upset or angry and Penelope had to remind her that she had to remain calm as much as possible, ESPECIALLY when it came to the cross-examination by the prosecutor. Penelope told Kris, "Kris, being upset because you are sad is one thing, and it is bound to happen, but try not to let your temper flair. The prosecution will take full advantage of that and show the jury how quickly you escalate, and how out of control you can be. Does that make sense? I am sure you have seen it in court before."

"I have and I understand what you are saying."

"Let's run through it again, and I will go over the list of witnesses we have when we finish."

They ran through the questions a couple more times, Kris doing much better each time. She kept her emotions in better check but teared up when recalling a few memories. She was getting better at talking about the rape, but there were certain aspects that still triggered her. She still found it difficult to describe in detail the events of that day, but she managed. Luckily, she would not have to do that unless the prosecution asked her. This was not about Mack and Shaen being on trial for their crime, it was about Kris fighting for her freedom for a crime she did NOT commit.

Penelope would not ask her to go into detail for multiple reasons, the biggest of which was to not provide the jury or prosecution any more of a motive for Kris to kill Mack. The prosecuting attorney already knew the details, and Penelope prayed he would not bring them up for that very reason. She was sure that if the prosecution did, the jury, after hearing all of what had been done to Kris, would have given them every reason to see Kris as being vengeful because of her inability to seek justice in the courts, which would have left Kris to seek her own justice.

They finished up early so Kris could get some sleep. "Kris, I will be here at about 6:30 on Monday morning. Court starts at 8 a.m. and we have to check in," Penelope told her.

"Okay. I will be ready … I think."

Ronnie told her she would be meeting them at the courts building. As the three climbed the stairs, Kris could hear laughter, and everyone appeared to be very relaxed. 'I am afraid to ask what is so funny." Kris said.

Tess spoke up, "Oh, we were just talking about your post-surgical antics, and how you asked everyone if they wanted to see your scars."

"Oh, good Lord. I know it was either you or Tony who brought that up. The only two people here right now who were in Virginia are the two of you."

"Well," Tess said, "There was the entire restaurant patio there too."

"I don't remember that, so, it must hot have happened," Kris laughed as she said it.

Tony and Tess looked at one another and at the same time, said, "Oh, yes, it did!"

Shaking her head with a grin on her face, Kris said, "I am going to bed. Y'all just keep making up stories about me—RUDE! She said good night and went to the back bedroom. Kris climbed into bed and, just as she was drifting off to sleep, heard footsteps coming down the hall. She opened her eyes and saw Tess's silhouette standing in the door.

"K.C., are you still awake?" Tess asked.

"Barely. What's up?"

"Adrienne is ready to go, so I came back to tell you good night."

"Oh, okay," Kris said as she was sitting up.

Tess leaned in to give Kris a hug, and when they broke the embrace, Tess put her hands on either side of Kris's face, leaned in and kissed her. It took no time at all before Kris was kissing Tess back. It was passionate, sensual, and extremely intimate—lasting at least two minutes. Kris's body was reacting as well. She could feel the butterflies in her stomach, heat rising into her face, and the overall excitement. When the kiss ended, Tess very gently kissed Kris's forehead. "I will see you soon sweetie. I am here if you need it."

"Thank you, Tess. It means the world to me that you came."

"That is what friends do. Love you, sweetie."

"Love you right back, Tess. I will see you soon. Kris fell back to sleep pretty relaxed as she dreamt of Tess.

CHAPTER 24

One evening Tony was working a late shift on the ship, and she went to Tess's house for an impromptu get-together. Everyone who came brought something to share, and different meats were cooked on the grill. Tess and her husband had a small pool and hot tub everyone could enjoy after dinner.

At some point during the evening, they were all sitting around the table talking when Tess's husband went up to a bedroom with a woman who was part of the swinger's group. For some reason, his leaving had upset Tess.

About 10 minutes after he had gone upstairs, Tess took Kris's hand and without saying a word, led her upstairs to the master bedroom. It was just the two of them, and when the door closed, Tess started kissing Kris. Soon after that, they were both on the bed, naked— exploring each other with their hands and mouths.

On Sunday, things were pretty low key around the house. Kris was getting her clothes ready for court. She had no clue exactly how many outfits she would need because she had no idea how long this was going to last. It could be a few days or a few weeks. Everything depended on how many witnesses each side had and breaks in the trial; there were multiple factors that played a part in the length of a trial. Tony ran out with Kris's dad, and while she was putting outfits together, Kris's mom came back to the bedroom. "Hey, baby girl."

"Hey Momma. Watcha doin?"

"I came back to talk to you. Are you okay?'"

"Yes. Why?"

"Kris, I am really concerned about you, about your marriage, and all the things you told us about. I don't understand why you would do those things."

"Are you referring to the swingers' stuff and friends I have made through it?"

"Are they really your friends though? How do you know you can depend on them?"

"Mom, I am fully aware you don't approve of what took place in my marriage. I did what I needed to, no, what I thought I needed to do to keep Tony and I together. He did not force me, threaten me, or manipulate me. I chose to do those things because I was trying to save my marriage. I made some good friends along the way too. Yes, I can depend on them. You see that Tess is here. She didn't come here for Tony or to stir anything up. She isn't trying to break up my marriage either."

"There is just something with the way she looks at you, and honestly, the way you look at her." Kris's mom told her.

"What are you talking about?" Kris asked.

"Look, you are my daughter, and I know the looks on your face pretty well. Do you have feelings for Tess?"

"No," Kris responded with a high pitch squeal in her voice.

"Well, that just said it all." Her mom said with a little playfulness behind it. "I know you and Tony are just going through the motions right now, and you have a lot more on your mind, but I think you really need to start thinking about who you are Baby Girl. Your daddy and I will always support you."

"Okay, Momma. I love you so much."

"I love you too. It's okay Kris, everything will be okay."

Kris's phone rang as she and her mom were hugging. She didn't recognize the number, but she answered anyway. "Hello?" she responded with a question in her tone.

The voice on the other end answered, "Hey Kris, its Derrick."

Kris recognized his voice right away. He didn't even have to tell her who it was. "What's going on Derrick?"

"I just wanted to tell you, if you didn't know already, I will be there in court tomorrow. I will be there for most of the trial, and I just wanted to give you a heads up."

"I did know, and I appreciate your telling me."

"How are you doing, babe?" he asked.

"I'm doing okay Derrick. I am scared shitless if you want to know the truth."

"I am sure you are, and nobody can blame you for that. It is going to all be okay, Kris. I truly believe that."

"Everyone keeps saying the same thing, but not one person is giving me any evidence to prove it."

They continued to chat about nonsense before ending the call and the remainder of the day was strictly family time. Penelope called Kris once to remind her what time she would be coming to get her in the morning. After the conversation ended, Kris, her parents, Tony, and her sisters had dinner together. After dinner, they all went down to the basement, lounged around, and watched movies. Kris fell asleep in the recliner, and when Tony tried to wake her to go upstairs to bed, she told him she wanted to stay in the basement and sleep there. It was cool, and she was comfortable enough that she could sleep through the night. Her sisters left, and everyone else went to bed. Kris was once again drifting off to sleep when her phone dinged with an incoming text message. It was Tess.

"Hey lady … are you doing okay?"

"Yes. Just drifting off to sleep. Your timing is impeccable."

"Sorry I can't be there with you," Tess said.

"Me too. I could use that little earlobe massage thing you do. It always relaxes me."

"Where are you right now?"

"I am in the basement. I am going to sleep in the recliner tonight."

"Are you alone?"

"Yes. Tony went upstairs to the bedroom."
"If I can get over there, would you like me to come see you for a bit?"

"You would need to be very quiet."

Tess sent a laughing emoji. "I think I can do that."

"Let me know," Kris said.

After about 10 minutes, Tess texted Kris and told her to unlock the basement door. A short time later, Tess quietly came through the door, sat on the other side of the reclining loveseat, and had Kris lay her head on her lap. Tess started rubbing Kris's temples and used her thumbs to rub from the center of her forehead out, very lightly.

Kris whispered, "Tess, I really do appreciate your coming here. It means a lot to me."

"I'm glad I could make it here for you, Kris. The other half isn't too happy about it, but I really don't care what he thinks at this point."

"Don't make me laugh. Mom will hear, and this would be difficult to explain," Kris said with a crooked smile.

"You know, when you smile like that, your eyes sparkle. It is mischievous and cute at the same time."

Kris reached up and took Tess's hand in hers. She brought Tess's hand to her lips and started to kiss the palm of her hand, then each finger. Tess leaned forward and slid her other hand from Kris's forehead, down the side of her neck, across her inner shoulder to where the neck and chest meat, and asked Kris, "How quiet can you be?"

"Pretty darn quiet, what about you?"

"As quiet as a church mouse," Tess replied as her hand slid further down and into Kris's shirt.

Kris sat up, her back against Tess's chest, turned her head and began to kiss her. They very quietly made love, not another word spoken between them until Tess was leaving. "I'll see you tomorrow, Kris. Get some sleep sweetie."

"You too, Tess. Be careful getting back."

CHAPTER 25

Kris's alarm went off at 5:30 a.m. She got up and walked upstairs. She started the shower, and stood under the hot water, relaxing more than she already was. At first, when she woke, she thought she dreamt of Tess coming over, but she could still smell her perfume in the blanket and on her pajama shirt. It was a perfect night, and as Kris stood there, under the heat and feeling the steam, she closed her eyes and replayed the encounter over and over until it was seared in her brain. *This may be the last time this will happen*, she thought to herself, and then she remembered she may be going to prison. *It wouldn't necessarily be the last time, just the last time it was that nice.* She corrected her own thoughts. By 6:30 a.m., Penelope was there and everyone else was ready to go. Ronnie, Adrienne, and Tess were all going together and would arrive about the same time.

On Monday morning, as Kris was getting ready at her parent's house, Richard was getting ready for court. He had to make one last stop to his office before the start of the trial and thought he would be the only one there, but Ingrid beat him there. Instead of having an intern gather the files and other necessary items, she and Richard decided it would be best if they were the only two handling the documents. Richard did not trust anyone other than Ingrid at this point in the game. "Are you ready for this?" he asked Ingrid.

"I surely don't think I have prepared enough. It is going to be a complete shit show as far as media attention is concerned, and the amount of people filling that courtroom is unreal," she replied.

"I know, but we will make it through. You are very good at what you do young lady, so I do not see something as simple as a crowd or the media scaring you easily. That is part of the reason why I told you what I did the other day. You get away from this office as soon as you are able. Promise me that this will be your last case with this office. I will make sure you have something better to go to after it is all said and done."

"Richard, you cannot make that promise."

"Ingrid, I can make that promise. I cannot tell you how, but I can tell you that you will have an amazing position available to you after this case. So, promise me."

"Okay, I promise. I will quit as soon as the gavel strikes," she said sheepishly.

"Thank you. You remind me so much of my daughter. I know how proud I would be of her, so your parents are probably equally as proud of you."

Ingrid walked closer to Richard and gave him a hug, "Thank you so much. It means the world to me that you hold me in such great company. I have heard so much about your daughter, and I am truly honored."

Richard could not help but tear up again. He had been doing a lot of that lately, but not nearly as much since he made the phone call. He only hoped that his daughter would be proud of him. Of all the times he could see his daughter do things to make him proud, he was just as eager to do the same. Even now, he did not want to disappoint the little girl he watched grow into the young woman she had become, until the day …

"Richard, are you still with me?" Ingrid asked.

"Yes, of course." He was so lost in his thoughts, he barely heard Ingrid repeatedly call his name.

"Do you want to double check and make sure I did not forget anything?" she asked.

"No ma'am. I have all the faith in the world in you Ingrid. I am so glad you are going to be by my side through this."

They completed their paperwork and gathered up the files. There was no turning back now. Richard was committed to his decision...

When Kris and everyone with her arrived at the court building, there was a mass of media outlets waiting at the bottom of the courthouse steps. If there wasn't a reporter, it was a police officer. Penelope looked at Kris as they were parking the car and asked, "Are you okay? You look like you are going to be sick."

"Do you think if I wait to throw up on one of the reporters, it will give me a couple of points in my favor with all the cops?"

Penelope was fully aware of how much cops hated the media, and while she would never dare say it, she was pretty sure the cops hated Kris more at this point. The worst part was they had no reason to hate Kris; they were mad at the wrong person. The lies being told to all of these officers provided the department with the opportunity for both the men and women to hate Kris, who was now an outsider and civilian. Had they looked further into Mack, and all the things he actually had done, and it had come to light Mack was drugging and raping women, it would only be the men who hated Kris. The women would be angry, but it more than likely would not be directed at Kris. And while the number of female officers was greatly shadowed by the number of male officers, the department as a whole did not want a group of their own mad at one person within the department.

As they walked toward the courthouse steps, Kris and Penelope were flanked by Tony and Kris's family and friends in addition to John Barker and six of John's friends who did corporate security. Despite all the people yelling at her, Kris felt quite safe. They climbed the steps leading up to the door, with protestors and police officers in uniform, most all of them with very angry looks on their faces but not saying a word. This demeanor from them all is what bothered Kris the most … that is until Tess spoke up.

"Good Lord. If there are this many cops here, who the fuck is doing their job?" She broke the tension quite quickly, making everyone giggle, which Kris would pay for later. Of course, as luck would have it, a photographer managed to get a picture of them all smiling, so the news headlines the following day inferred that Kris and everyone in her group were making a mockery of Mack's death. As they finally made it to the top of the steps, some of the female officers, all dressed in their formal police uniform, came from between the officers in the front row, stepped over the mesh fencing and followed Kris into the courtroom. Leading the group of women, which was a handful of people at best, was her old partner, Wanda. Kris didn't know a lot of the other women, but that did not matter. There were officers lined up inside the courthouse as well and stepping out from the first part of this line, was Andrew, who fell in step right next to Wanda. Kris was already overwhelmed, but this was different. She was overwhelmed by the love and support she was being given, not by the stress of this entire situation.

They entered the long hallway and walked to the courtroom. Penelope and Kris put their files and jackets at the table and when they finished getting settled, Penelope turned to Kris's family and said, "We have to go downstairs and check in. It should not take too long." Kris's family, Tess, Adrienne, Ronnie, and Trixie, as well as John and the crew helping to protect her, sat down in the rows behind the defense table. In the 10 minutes it took for them to check in and walk back into the courtroom, the defense side of the gallery had filled up. Kris started to tear up. All of her childhood friends, teachers from grade school through college, and her former neighbor from Virginia. *If I come out of this okay, it will take me a lifetime to thank them all,* Kris thought. She was floored at how many people showed up for her. Then, as Kris and Penelope walked to the table, she suddenly felt very uncomfortable. While she was overwhelmed by the support she did have, when Kris looked over to the other side of the gallery, she noticed the sea of blue. It looked like every officer who worked for the City of St. Louis had shown up.

Penelope acknowledged Richard and Ingrid's presence as they were sitting down. They nodded their heads at Penelope when Richard said, "Counselor, it is not too late to take a deal. Do you really want to put Mrs. Parker through this?"

Penelope looked at Kris, Kris leaned in and whispered to Penelope, "If the judge isn't here yet, can I flip him off?" Penelope laughed very loudly and was still giggling when she told Richard, "She said she will decline the offer."

CHAPTER 26

The bailiff stepped forward to address the courtroom. In a loud voice he said, "ALL RISE!" He continued his announcement as the judge walked in. As soon as the judge sat, so did everyone else in the courtroom. The judge asked if there were any last-minute motions or questions for either side. Both Penelope and Richard said "No." The judge told the bailiff to bring in the potential jurors. Richard looked at the panel of jurors, figuring out who he would not exclude or challenge. The plan he made a few days ago was already in motion, so he wasn't going to stress about making sure there would be jurors ready to convict Kris. There were 20 people sitting in the courtroom as potential jurors, and Penelope and Richard both knew the list would dwindle down quickly.

The judge introduced himself and began to go over courtroom etiquette, explaining to them that if an answer to a question posed by either side was too sensitive in nature to say out loud, that they were to raise their hand and ask to approach to discuss it with the judge and the attorneys. The judge asked some preliminary questions, "Is there anything about this trial, such as the potential length of time, daily schedule that presents a problem for you in the ability to serve on this jury?" Six hands went up; however, only two people were excused from the panel. "Does anyone know a member of my staff, the counselors, or another member of the jury?" No hands went up. This continued for another 15 minutes with the judge, and then it was Penelope's turn.

She stood up and addressed the jury, "Ladies and gentlemen, I want to thank you for showing up today, as I know you do not have a choice in the matter. I am going to ask a few questions, and please answer them with honesty, because there is no penalty for a truthful answer. I know this has been in the news, and hard to avoid seeing or hearing about, so I would like to know if any of you have been a victim or have had a close family member become a victim of a violent crime?"

Two hands went up, so Penelope asked the nature of the crime and the outcome of the cases. She thanked and excused the two jurors, expecting a challenge that never came. Surely Richard would have wanted someone who was quick to convict Kris. Richard stood up and looked at the jurors, "Ladies and gentlemen, first let me thank you for sacrificing your time to be here. As my colleague across the aisle pointed out, you did not have a choice in the matter and are more than likely thinking, *They are both right, I did not have a choice and it isn't their fault I was too stupid to get out of jury duty before this process started.*" With that comment, the entire courtroom made a sound of some sort, most of them stifling a giggle, but Richard's boss was not a happy man when he heard that.

"Counsel, please approach the bench," the judge requested. Richard could see it was taking everything in the judge's power to keep his voice calm. As he reached the bench, the judge looked at him and said, "Counselor, you need to apologize to the jury panel. I cannot even believe I have to have this discussion with you. That remark was uncalled for and WAY out of line."

"Yes, Your Honor." Richard turned and Penelope could see a smirk on his face. He wasn't sorry at all. "I am going to try this again. Ladies and gentlemen, I sincerely thank you for your sacrifice for attending this court today. Please accept my apologies. As you can imagine, I am under a tremendous amount of stress and have lost myself for a moment. The defense and I have a few more questions for you until we reach the necessary number of jurors." There were some nods of acknowledgement in accepting his apology from most of them, but he could see the faces of some panel members and they were less than pleased with his comment. He questioned one of the angry jurors individually, "Sir, could you state your juror number, occupation, and how long you have been at that occupation?" The man stated his number and advised the court he was an engineer for a major company that designs and builds military aircraft. Richard had to keep this one, especially since he was going to keep slipping in the digs.

"Have any of you studied or practiced law?" One younger member of the panel stated she was currently in law school. "What type of law are you studying?" Richard inquired.

"Contract law," she replied. There was no reason why she couldn't remain on the jury, and Penelope did not challenge.

Both Richard and Penelope continued to pose questions, finally asking "Please bear in mind that not every criminal case will have DNA evidence, video, or a "smoking gun" if you will. Given that information, if you are selected to this jury, would any of you be unable or unwilling to render a verdict based solely on the evidence presented at trial?" That was the question that brought the panel down to 12 jurors and one alternate juror should something happen to a primary.

The court took a brief recess, and Richard turned to Ingrid. "Are you ready for your opening statement?"

"I think so. I'm not going to lie; I am pretty nervous about this," she replied.

"Of course, you are, but you are going to do great." He patted her on the shoulder and helped her get ready.

Across the aisle, Penelope was talking with Kris about why there were no challenges to the jurors. "I would sure like to know what is going on in Richard's head." Penelope said to Kris. "He has always had challenges and sometimes selection takes hours. Something is going on, and I want to know what it is."

"Do you think it means something bad for me?" Kris asked her.

"Oddly, no, I don't."

The judge returned to the courtroom and addressed Richard and Ingrid. "Do the people wish to make an opening statement?"

Ingrid stood, "We do your honor. Ladies and gentlemen of the jury, as you all know, we are here today because a former member of the St. Louis Metropolitan Police Department, Mack Parkins, was found behind the flood wall dead, and had, at minimum, been physically assaulted. Before succumbing to his injuries, it was discovered that Mr. Parkins had been tied up, beaten, anally penetrated by a foreign object, and left there like trash. The people will show through documents, phone calls, and witness statements that the only person who had the means, motive, and opportunity to commit such an act was the defendant, Kristine Parker. We will show that Mrs. Parker's desire for revenge developed as the result of her need to get justice for an alleged rape which she accused Mack Parkins of committing. The only way for this justice, in her mind, was to kill him, but not before making him suffer the way she alleges she suffered at his hands."

Ingrid continued, "The People will show that Mrs. Parker had the means and opportunity to commit this act due to her knowledge of the area, her knowledge of the law, and her ability to hide in plain sight. She had an opportunity every time she came to town for a visit, but nothing happened to Mr. Parkins until AFTER Mrs. Parker learned she was unable to file criminal charges against him for the alleged rape. Now, the defense will say that Mrs. Parker could not have committed this crime because she was in a meeting with a civil litigation attorney, with her family, or a friend at the time of the assault resulting in Mr. Parkins' death. The truth is, ladies and gentlemen, we do not know exactly when this took place, we only know the last time he was alive based on his cell phone records and what day he was found. Knowing that there was some time in between, how are we supposed to believe that Mrs. Parker NEVER had the opportunity to commit this horrible act that led to the death of one of St. Louis's finest officers?"

"After reviewing the evidence, and listening to witnesses, you, ladies, and gentlemen of the jury, will have no other choice than to render a verdict of guilty." The People will prove to you that the defendant, Kristine Parker, is guilty of murder in the second degree and tampering with evidence. Thank you for your time ladies and gentlemen, and on behalf of my colleague, I want to apologize for Richard calling you all stupid. Clearly that is not the case."

As she walked away, she saw Richard nod his approval, also knowing that the last comment did nothing more than remind the jury as to what they are thought of by attorneys.

CHAPTER 27

Penelope stood up, and addressed the jury, "Ladies and gentlemen of the jury. I want to thank you for your time and sacrifice. You have a very heavy, difficult task ahead of you, and quite frankly, I do not envy you. You are going to be given the burden of deciding who, between myself and the prosecution, has presented the best case, the best evidence, the best witnesses, and the best experts, culminating in deciding, 'beyond a reasonable doubt' as to whether or not Mrs. Parker is guilty of the crimes she has committed. The prosecution has already told you they are going to present evidence in the form of witnesses, documents, and phone calls that will point to the guilt of my client. What the prosecution did not tell you is that all of this evidence is circumstantial. Phone calls and overheard conversations by witnesses have been taken out of context and are incomplete at best.

"Please, ladies and gentlemen of the jury, keep in mind that it is up to the prosecution to bear the burden of proof of Mrs. Parker's guilt. It is completely up to them to present this evidence proving that Mrs. Parker and ONLY Mrs. Parker wanted Mack Parkins dead and in fact killed him. While it is up to them to prove this to you, it is up to me to make sure my client is not wrongfully convicted of crimes she did not commit. I, too, will provide you with witnesses, documents, and copies of phone records showing that Mrs. Parker was not the only person with the means, motive, or opportunity to commit such a horrendous act, but that she was nowhere near the area of where Mack Parkins was found. Some of the witnesses testifying for the prosecution are questionable at best, the physical evidence will not prove absolute guilt, let alone 'beyond a reasonable doubt.' After presenting my case, you will have no other choice than to render a verdict of not guilty. Mrs. Parker is not the scorned lover, the vengeful victim, or the sadistic killer she is being painted to be by the prosecution, the victim's family, or members of the St. Louis Metropolitan Police Department, and that is something I have every intention of proving to you. Thank you again for your time."

As Richard listened to Penelope, he was watching the jury. He could see the doubt on their faces, especially when she mentioned the evidence being circumstantial, having proof that Kris was nowhere near the area where Mack was found, affording her the opportunity to kill Mack. She was not wrong about anything—the physical evidence did not really prove Kris killed him. His witnesses consisted of a drunk homeless man who did not even know what year it was, but the police found his story of seeing the entire thing credible. Richard's boss insisted he would be placed on the witness list. The police department wanted something done, and Richard's boss was making sure it happened. Penelope pointed all of this out to the jury.

She was on a roll and her opening statement lasted for nearly five minutes. *Damn, she is good.* As he continued to listen to her, he wondered if anyone caught the fact that Ingrid made statements of an absolute nature. Not one time did Ingrid use the term "beyond a reasonable doubt," so in some ways, she was planting doubt in the minds of jurors as well, provided they actually caught on to what she had said.

Ingrid was sitting next to Richard, looking at him, and still in disbelief at the comment Richard made to the potential jurors about being stupid. *What the hell is wrong with him?* she asked herself. That was a move unlike anything she had ever seen or heard from Richard. His overall behavior was completely out of character for Richard as well. She could tell he did not really care what happened, and if she could tell, surely others could too. She prayed that nobody else could see what she was seeing. They were both going to hear about the "stupid" remark from the boss. When Penelope finished, as she walked past the table, Ingrid saw Richard bow slightly at the waist, acknowledging the wonderful opening statement she had given.

It was getting late in the afternoon, and the judge called a recess for the day. He reminded the jurors not to discuss the case with anyone, not to read any newspapers, or any other media outlet that would influence them in the case. Richard packed up the files and told Ingrid to go ahead and go home, that he would take care of everything. As Richard was driving out of the parking garage, he was sure he saw the judge talking with a couple of detectives that had been in the courtroom.

The first witness for the prosecution was a woman who had been at lunch when she saw Kris and another woman leaning across the table to be in closer proximity of each other to keep their conversation private. The woman testified to overhearing Kris and the woman she was with, mention Mack's name a couple of times, alluding to his death. She repeated Kris's words verbatim "Get in line, it is pretty long at this point." Penelope shot out of her chair objecting to the statement, citing that Kris was referring to a long list of other people who would also want to see Mack dead. During her cross examination, Penelope was able to get the witness to admit that just because the conversation may have alluded to Mack's premature death, it did not mean Kris was the person that made it happen. Penelope finished her cross examination, Richard watching the reaction of the jury. They were all taking notes, especially when Penelope pointed out the possibility of an even longer line of suspects.

Richard called a couple of other witnesses who had overheard Kris in conversation with other people. Almost everyone testifying to hearing Kris's conversations, also stated that they heard Kris mention an alleged rape, Mack's name, and his premature death. Once again, Penelope was sure to point out that Kris may have mentioned the murder, but she was not necessarily the one to make it happen. Richard's next witness testified to hearing Kris and her parents at the casino the same day she found out criminal charges could not be filed, but it was Kris's dad whose words he discussed. Richard asked the man to elaborate on what he heard and saw.

"I parked a couple of spots down from the defendant's car, but there were spaces open, I could see her sitting in her car as she took a phone call. After a couple of minutes, I saw her put her phone down and her head on the steering wheel."

"And then what happened?" Richard asked.

"I saw her get out of the car. Her dad hugged her, and I could hear her sobbing."

"How long did it take to gain her composure?"

"A couple of minutes. When her dad stopped hugging her, he put his hands on her shoulders and looked at her. This is when I heard him say, 'Don't you worry Baby Girl, Daddy will take care of everything.

It will not take long to sight in my rifles.' I then heard Kris tell him to stop, that 'neither of those assholes was worth going to jail over."

"Did he reply to her?"

"He did. He said he would not do anything she did not want him to or that would cause her more issues, but the look on her dad's face said otherwise."

Richard could see Penelope getting ready to stand up. He knew what he had just done and was okay with it. "How do you mean, sir?"

"Well, he looked at Mrs. Parker's mom, and I took that to mean he was still going to kill Mack."

With that, Penelope jumped up and objected to the testimony being pure speculation. She asked if the witness was a body language or facial expression expert, which she knew he wasn't. The judge sustained the objection and told Richard to rephrase the question. When he did, Richard asked with only a slight difference, and when he did it a third time, Penelope did not even stand up. This time, she spread her arms out, asking the judge if she should just remain standing. Richard was getting a kick out of it, but when he looked over at his boss, he could see anger spread across his face, which is exactly what Richard was looking for. He was also fully aware of the fact that this witness, his witness, just provided the jury with an enormous amount of doubt as to Kris's guilt. In all reality, he should have been a witness for the defense, since the conversation between Kris and her father made her father look more guilty than it did her.

"Counselor," the judge addressed Richard, "I think it is best if you move on with this line of questioning."

"Yes, Your Honor. I am finished with this witness."

Penelope stood up halfway and told the judge she did not have any questions for the witness. He instructed Richard to call his next witness. "Your honor, the People would like to call Detective Shaen Finney to the stand."

As Shaen entered the courtroom and walked towards the bench, Kris immediately reacted to seeing him for the first time in nearly 20 years.

CHAPTER 28

*R*onnie *slid the photo over to Kris, and for the first time in almost 20 years, she laid eyes on Shaen.* She started crying and shaking, and after about 30 seconds, leaned to the side where a court officer was standing not far behind her and threw up. *It took everything she had to keep her composure.* As all of this was happening, Shaen had a smirk on his face that Richard wished he could wipe off with a punch to Shaen's mouth. Richard would, however, make that smirk disappear fairly soon. *Ronnie raised an eyebrow, and Kris shook her head in the affirmative as she pointed to Shaen's face in the class photo. Ronnie bumped Kris's arm with her elbow, indicating she would talk more openly when they left the building.*

When Kris threw up, a recess was immediately taken. This time Shaen was taken out the door leading to the judge's chambers. Penelope and members of Kris's family and friends consoled her. They were not helping much, but when Richard saw a tall, beautiful blonde woman walk up, everyone backed away from Kris. She took Kris's hands and looked right into her eyes. As the woman spoke, Richard could see Kris taking deep breaths, finally pulling it together. Richard later learned that the woman was Kris's therapist, Adrienne Shiffer; however, the way they were looking at each other, he got the impression there was something more to their relationship. He may have to explore that when it came time for Adrienne's testimony.

When the half hour recess was over, and the floor had been cleaned, the courtroom filled back up. The judge came back in, and Richard called Shaen to the stand. When Shaen sat down, he looked directly at Kris with a smirk. Richard was starting to turn red with anger at Shaen's behavior. "Detective, please state your name and title for the record."

"I am Detective Shaen Finney, and I am a detective with a municipal police department within St. Louis County."

"Have you always worked for your current department?"

"No sir. I was also an officer for the St. Louis Metropolitan Police Department."

"And how long did you work there?"

"I went into the academy in 1996 and left the department in 2011."

"Detective, did you know Mack Parkins?"

"I did."

"How did you know him?"

"He was my field training officer on occasion. I only rode with him when my regular training officer was off for some reason."

"Detective, do you know the defendant?"

"Yes, I do."

"And how do you know Mrs. Parker?"

"She was a police officer for St. Louis Police Department as well. She graduated a couple of years before me. She worked in the same station house but different districts than I did."

"And did you ever work directly with the defendant?"

"If you mean did I ever patrol with her, then the answer is no. Mrs. Parker was in District 4 and I was in District 9."

"Did you only interact with her at work?"

"No."

"Can you tell me more about your outside interactions with her?" Richard asked.

"She was hooking up with Mack."

"Hooking up?"

"Yes. To put it bluntly, they were sleeping together … a lot. Mack would have me sit at the entrance to an alley so I could make sure nobody would see them together."

"These hook ups took place while you were on duty?"

"Yes, of course. We only hung out a couple of times off duty," Shaen stated.

"Under what circumstances did these interactions take place?"

"Just an after shift get together here and there."

"Do you only know the defendant from these interactions?"

"Yes."

"So, these interactions were only when you were tagging along with her and Mack?"

"No."

Richard could see Shaen's expression change in an instant. He did not like being looked at as a third wheel. It brought a sense of satisfaction to Richard to see Shaen's smirk disappear from his face. "Detective, were you a tag-along or was there more to your interactions with the defendant?"

Shaen answered the question through gritted teeth and a red face. "I wasn't a 'tag-along;' we all hung out together after work."

"Did you ever have a sexual encounter with the defendant? Don't forget you are under oath Detective ..." Richard turned towards the gallery because he knew Shaen's wife was in the courtroom. He turned back before Shaen could answer.

"Well Detective?"

"Yes. I did."

"How many times?" Richard turned back towards the gallery to watch Shaen's wife.

"Just the one time."

"Was it just you and the defendant or was anyone else with you during the one-time sexual encounter?"

"There was someone else."

"Tell me Detective, who was that someone else?"

"Mack Parkins," Shaen answered.

Richard looked once again at Shaen's wife, whose face was beet red with anger. He could see the veins popping from her temples.

"Was this encounter planned?"

Shaen looked like he wanted to shrink into a dark hole at this point. "What do you mean by planned?"

"Did you all get off work one day and plan to go have sex?"

"No."

"So how did you come to have sex with her that one time?"

"We had all worked the overnight shift and the following morning after shift change, we went to CODE 40. It had been a particularly rough night for all of us, and we went for food and drinks," Shaen explained.

"At 7 a.m.?"

"Yes, the bar was owned by two former police officers, so it opened for the night shift crews as well."

"Please continue." Richard could see that Shaen was a little more comfortable with this path of questioning, simply because it was making Kris look to be a slut. The smirk on his face was still gone though.

"We were sitting at the bar…"

"Who is 'we'?" Richard asked.

"Kris, Mack, and me. In that seating order."

"Thank you. Continue please."

"We were sitting at the bar talking about the events of that night and Kris was pounding the drinks pretty quickly."

"Do you remember what she was drinking?"

"Something with hard alcohol."

"Were you drinking as well?"

"Yes. I was drinking bottled beer."

"Okay. What happened next?"

"Kris got up to go to the bathroom but not before ordering another drink. When she was out of eyesight, Mack took her car keys from the bar."

Shaen was a bit of a smooth talker too. He knew exactly what to say to get what he wanted, making the person he was manipulating think it was their idea. He was sitting in one of his lecture halls one afternoon when he saw the teaching assistant come through the door just moments before the professor. Both looked disheveled and harried, like they had just woken up.

They just got out of bed or something, he was thinking. He could tell the two had been together, and now he was going to capitalize on it.

There weren't many people in the lecture hall yet, and those who were did not pay attention to what was going on down at the front with the T.A. and professor. Shaen picked up his things and moved down the aisle to the front of the classroom.

"Is everything okay?" the T.A. asked.

Shaen noticed that one of her shirt buttons had been ripped off. "Yes. Why do you ask?"

"You usually sit toward the back. Do you have a question or need something explained?"

It was a statistics class, so he always needed something explained. He was struggling in the class and trying to keep a passing grade.

"I have a question, but I won't ask it here," he told her.

"Let me get the professor's calendar, and I will see what he has open for office hours."

"The question is for you, not him," Shaen said.

"Oh, um, okay." The T.A. walked to Shaen and stood in front of him.

"Let's go out to the hallway."

She followed him out of the lecture hall and down the hallway toward the bathrooms. There was a small hallway leading to a maintenance room that was rarely used. He led her down to that area and stopped, motioning her to go past him.

"So. Here is the deal—I know you are having sex with the professor which is probably how you got the T.A. position. If you don't want me to tell anyone, you are going to make sure I not only get a better grade in the class, but you are going to have sex with me too."

"Excuse me? I have absolutely no clue what you are talking about."

"Don't play with me. I saw you both walking in, and your button is ripped off your shirt."

"That happened the other day, and I forgot about it until I was on my way here. I was closer to class than I was my apartment."

Shaen stepped closer to her, backing her into the wall. He leaned into her and whispered, "You are going to fuck me, or I am going to the Dean of Students."

A tear started to roll down her cheek, and she succumbed to his demands. "Fine, whatever you say." And she started to walk away.

"Oh no. We are going to solidify this…" he undid his jeans and pulled his semi-hard penis out.

"…You are going to take care of me with your mouth before class."

She did what she was told, and he finished in her mouth. As she stood up, he put his hand lightly at her throat. "Oh, and you are going to make sure I get at least a 'B' in this class. I think an 'A' would be too obvious."

She replied with a head nod and went back into the lecture hall. Shaen developed a smirk on his face as he walked back into the hall. The T.A. and the professor were talking again, both looking at Shaen as he walked in. 'So, she told her bed buddy?' he thought. 'That's fine because he isn't going to narc on me, not unless he wants to lose his job.'

The more he looked at her, Shaen began to think about how much she looked like his mom. This got him stirring again, but it had more to do with the idea of having control over someone like his mom than any sexual component. 'At least I can get her to do what I want and need. If Mom would have done what I needed, her brother wouldn't have ever laid a hand on me.'

He finally had control over something in his life—something he could dictate the outcome to.

Any time he was in a class he was struggling with; Shaen would figure out a way to manipulate the situation. Nine times out of 10, he would manipulate and blackmail an older woman. Some of them were students, and some were professors. He chose his target and then watched for a while to see what he could use against them. His senior year in college, his focus was normally on the professors, but there were a few T. A.'s and other graduate students set in his sights too.

By doing this, he managed to make it through his hardest classes with a "B" as his final grade. He would throw an "A" in there for some of the classes, but not often because he did not want it to look suspicious. He made sure he attended the study sessions the T.A. ran, so it looked like he was taking his studies seriously.

CHAPTER 29

Did Mack say anything to you about the keys?"

"Yes." He said he would have to take Kris home and get her car before the shift that night."

"Did Mrs. Parker argue with Mack about it?"

"No. She was fine with it."

"Tell me, what, if anything happened after that?"

"By this time, she was so drunk, she could barely stand up," Shaen said.

"Anything else?"

"Yes. She was all over Mack and me."

"Define 'all over.'" Richard instructed.

"She was kissing us, grabbing us, and telling us both how much she wanted to have sex with us, but did not use those words. It was more vulgar than that."

"And tell me Detective, did you oblige?"

"No. When we finished drinking, we went and got something else to eat and to get some coffee in her."

Richard knew this was a complete lie, but he was biding his time. "Did that help her?"

"Yes. She was walking and talking much better. She was still tipsy but was more with it."

"By 'with it', do you mean she was able to drive home?"

"No. Mack still did not want her to drive."

"Then what exactly do you mean by 'with it'?"

"I mean she could coherently answer questions and her decision-making skills were more intact."

"Oh, so what you are saying is that she was able to consent to sex."

"Yes."

"And did she?"

"No," Shaen answered. When he realized what he said, he clarified. "Excuse me, I meant 'no' as in we didn't ask her to have sex; she asked us."

"Was she still 'all over you' at this time?" Richard inquired.

"No," Shaen replied. "We had an actual discussion about it."

"You discussed having sex?"

"Yes. She told us that she had always had a fantasy of being with two men at the same time and that she would rather it be with two men she knew and could trust."

"So then, you and Mack were in the position to be the ones to consent, not the defendant?"

"I guess so, yes."

"Detective Finney, were you intoxicated at this point?"

"Absolutely not. I lost my buzz quite some time before the conversation took place."

"So, you consented to the sex?"

"Yes. Mack and I both agreed to it. We would have been stupid not to take her up on the offer."

Richard turned at the very moment Shaen's wife ran out of the courtroom. Now, it was Richard's turn to smirk. By this time, Shaen's face was a deep red.

"What happened after that?"

"After what?"

"After the conversation detailing her fantasy?" Richard asked.

"Do you want the details?" Shaen asked.

"No. I don't believe that is necessary," Richard replied. "You can just give a big highlight."

"When we finished the conversation, we went back to Mack's house and had sex."

"Do you know how Mrs. Parker got home?"

"Yes. Mack ended up taking her home, but first he drove me to her car, which I drove to her apartment while Mack followed. Once we dropped her car off, Mack took me back to my car at his house. I left and went to sleep before my shift that night."

"How were things at work that night?"

"Kris ended up calling in sick, but between Mack and I, they were fine. I do know that when she did come back, things were a little awkward. By the end of the following week, Mack had cut things off with Kris completely."

"Are you referring to their physical relationship?"

"Yes."

"Thank you, detective Finney. I have nothing further for this witness."

Penelope stood up and approached the witness box. "Good morning, Detective."

"Morning," Shaen replied with disdain in his voice.

"You said you only hung out with my client a couple of times. Is that correct?"

"Yes, it is."

"Did you have sex with my client more than once?"

"I already said that it was just the one time."

"That's right. And this one-time sexual encounter with my client was with Mack Parkins as well, correct?"

"Yes."

"And it was completely consensual on Mrs. Parker's end, correct?"

"That is correct."

"I am a little confused, because when Mr. McCullen asked you if my client was able to consent to sex, you instantly said 'no' and then backed out of that statement pretty quickly."

"That is correct, because she initiated the conversation about a threesome. I misunderstood the question the first time."

"But Detective, if Mrs. Parker was still 'tipsy,' as you said she was, how are you so sure she was in the right frame of mind to consent to sex?" Penelope asked.

"She wasn't still tipsy."

"Then why was it necessary for Mack to drive her home when your encounter was over?"

Shaen started to stammer finding the answer and couldn't produce one. "I guess he just wanted to be safe."

"I see, so she was NOT able to consent?"

"Yes. She initiated the conversation about the threesome."

"Did Mrs. Parker tell you or Mack that she wanted to have that threesome THAT day?"

"Sort of," He replied.

"Sort of? What does that mean? Detective, she either said yes or no."

"As I stated earlier, she told us she had a fantasy about being with two men at the same time."

"But she NOT say she wanted to fulfill that fantasy that THAT day, did she Detective?"

"No. I guess she didn't."

"So that brings me back to my original question … did she consent to have sex with you and Mack?"

"No," Shaen replied through gritted teeth and a very red face.

"Tell me something Detective Finney, if someone walks into your station and reported that two men had sex with them after they had been drinking, and drinking to the point where it wasn't 'safe' to drive home, what charges would be filed on the two men?"

"At minimum, sexual assault of some degree."

"Exactly."

"But she did not say 'no' either."

"Did she say 'Yes, let's do this right here, right now on this day,' or was it simply a statement to open the possibility to having a threesome?"

"She didn't."

"She didn't what, Detective?"

Shaen was most certainly not smirking anymore. Richard watched the panic spread across his face, sweat beading on his forehead, and Shaen looked to him to object on something, anything at this point.

"Detective, what didn't Mrs. Parker do?"

"She didn't say she wanted to do anything that day, but she did consent because she never said she didn't want to do a threesome that day."

"How very archaic of you to justify it all. Did it ever occur to you that Mrs. Parker did not say 'no' because she was too drugged up or intoxicated to say much of anything?"

"No, it didn't because —"

Penelope cut him off, "I have nothing further for this witness."

CHAPTER 30

Everyone was waiting for Ingrid to re-direct, but she had been instructed by Richard not to. She was confused, but he reassured her he knew what he was doing. She stood and said, "We have nothing further for this witness."

Nobody could figure out what the hell was happening and why Richard was so cavalier about the entire trial. Their boss was fuming and had been from the very start. Richard called Cathy next. Shaen left the courtroom after Penelope finished with him. She wasn't as aggressive as Richard thought she would be, but it was just enough to get him flustered and sow the seeds of doubt deeper in the jury's minds. Cathy told the court how she knew Mack, Shaen, and Kris.

"Did you recognize Mrs. Parker when she walked into the Records Division?"

"Not right away. It was her voice I recognized. That is when I was able to put a name to a face."

"What had she come to your department for?"

"She requested a copy of the police report she filed against Mack."

"What were the allegations?"

"She filed a rape report."

"And did you provide Mrs. Parker a copy of that report?"

"No," Cathy responded.

"Why not?" Richard prayed that she would answer the way he thought she should. They were in a rhythm in the question and answer, like a tennis match.

"When I pulled the file up, there was a flag on it and stated to contact our supervisor before releasing a copy."

"So, you are telling me you violated the Sunshine Law?"

"No, I did not."

"Was the investigation into the rape still open?"

"No."

"Then you violated the Sunshine Law."

"Not exactly," Cathy responded.

"How did you 'not exactly' violate the Sunshine Law?"

"I was told not to provide a copy to Mrs. Parker."

"By whom?"

"I already said, my supervisor."

"Who told your supervisor to refuse a copy to Mrs. Parker?"

"Someone higher up in the department I guess."

"Why would they do that?" Richard asked.

"I was told the investigation was still ongoing."

"You JUST said it was not ongoing."

"I don't know then. Clearly, I was not privy to everything the top floor does," Cathy said with a quip.

"Or you don't know your job," Richard said before stating he was done with the witness.

Penelope was making notes when the questioning was turned over to her.

"Good afternoon," Penelope said.

"Hello," Cathy replied.

Penelope could tell Cathy thought she was better than everyone else. While they were sitting at the table during Richard's questioning, Kris filled her in on how Cathy was when she worked with her. Penelope started her questioning, "Did you know the decedent, Mack Parkins as well?"

"I did."

"How did you know him?"

"Prior to moving to the Records Division, Mack, Detective Finney, and Mrs. Parker, and I worked in the same station. They were officers, and I worked behind the desk."

"Did you have an occasion to work more closely with Mack?"

"Yes."

"When was that?"

"When he was on light duty following a surgery."

"How would you describe your relationship with Mack?"

"We became good friends. We confided in each other."

"Is there anything in particular he confided in you?"

"Yes. He told me about his sexual relationship between him and Mrs. Parker."

"Did you know he was married?"

"Yes, and so did Mrs. Parker. She didn't care."

"Your Honor, I would like to have that last statement stricken from the record. This witness is not a mind reader and cannot speak to how Mrs. Parker felt."

"The jury will disregard that last remark, and it will be stricken from the record."

"What, if any concerns, did you have about Mack being in this relationship?"

"I was concerned about Mack because Kris was not stable."

"Your honor…" Penelope did not have to finish, as the judge warned Cathy and once again instructed the jury to disregard the comment and have it stricken.

"Let's try this again. Why were you concerned about Mack?"

"It was well known around the department that Kris could not be trusted."

"Why is that?"

"She had already put her training officer in hot water. Since she had been with the department, three veteran officers had been investigated. Nobody trusted her enough to be around her more than necessary and Mack chose to spend even more time with her. He needed to be aware of the games she played. She had some sort of magic spell over him."

There were a few snickers from the gallery as well as from the jury box. Even Richard and Ingrid had a hard time stifling a laugh. Cathy sounded like she was testifying at the Salem Witch Trials, and Kris was putting spells on men to seduce them. Penelope put her head down to hide her giggle. "Were you jealous of their relationship?"

"No. I had no reason to be."

"You didn't feel anything OTHER than friendship for Mack?"

"No."

"I see. Did you keep in contact with Mack after he left the department?"

"From time to time, yes."

"Did you speak to him during the time period my client was filing the criminal charges or after?"

"No."

"Are you sure?" Penelope asked as she was walking to the table to pick up copies of the phone records. "I have a large list of phone records that I am sure say otherwise."

"You will not find my phone number, or the number from the office calling, or getting calls from Mack Parkins."

"That is because you used a burner phone. Nothing further, your honor."

CHAPTER 31

The judge called a recess until the following morning at 8:00 a.m. Richard watched the gallery empty before he left himself. As Kris exited the courtroom, he saw another woman flank Kris's left side. She was slightly shorter and had long dark hair. She had her hand on the small of Kris's back and he could swear that at some point, saw the woman's hand slide to Kris's butt and give a brief rub and pat. Kris turned to her left, profile showing, and Richard could see pure joy on her face.

Richard and Ingrid's boss was waiting for Richard when he left the courtroom. He was not a happy man. "Richard, I don't know what the HELL you are doing, but it looks a lot like sabotage. I told you how this case needs to end, and it will be your career if it doesn't."

"Don't worry boss, I promise you, this will end the way it is supposed to."

"IT BETTER!" he yelled and stormed out of the courtroom.

"Are you okay Richard?" Ingrid asked. She had been standing in a position that prevented Richard from seeing her.

Richard laughed and said, "Oh my God, yes. I honestly could not be better. Do not worry about me. Like I just told the boss, everything will turn out the way it is supposed to."

"Richard, please be careful. I don't want you to lose your job."

"That will not happen. They are not going to fire me, Ingrid. I promise," he reassured her.

"I surely hope not." She spoke, "See you tomorrow."

"See you tomorrow, Ingrid." As he walked to his car, his phone rang. "Hey. I was just going to call you. Yes, I decided I will do it before closing statements. Okay, see you then."

Things were shaking up around the courthouse. Shaen's wife was not there the following day. Richard had heard she had left the house with the kids. They had not been married at the time of Kris's rape, but

Shaen and his wife were living together and newly engaged. Richard's boss was watching his every move. The next witness called by the prosecution was the medical examiner. The injuries sustained by Mack were described in detail. The Chief Medical Examiner was a very well-known Forensic Pathologist. She testified to the fact that Mack had suffered from multiple fractures to the ribs, legs, and arms. She also described a couple of open wounds believed to have been made by a sharp object. Richard was doing the questioning this time.

"Doctor, what was Mack Parkins' primary cause of death?"

"The cause of death is listed as being sepsis secondary to blunt and sharp force trauma."

"And the manner of death?"

"The manner of death is homicide."

"Thank you. Your witness counselor," he said as he turned to Penelope.

"Doctor, thank you for being here today. You ruled the manner of death being homicide, but does that mean that the person who inflicted all of that trauma leading to Mack Parkins' death was without a doubt, my client?"

"Of course, it doesn't. Quite honestly it is not something I look for even if it were possible to determine. I strictly document my findings of the post-mortem exam."

"At what point does your documentation start?" Penelope asked.

"My documentation begins with my post-mortem exam of the victim; however, the entire case file documentation begins with an investigator who works for my office."

"Is that investigator a police officer?"

"No. The medical examiner investigator is completely separate from the police department."

"Will you walk me through the steps of a case from start to finish?"

"Sure. Our office takes calls from various entities such as hospice nurses and hospitals as well as police officers who are required to report the death of an individual based on the circumstances under which they died. In this case, an investigator received a call from the police department when Mr. Parkins was found. The investigator would respond to the scene and work in conjunction with the police department; however, they do not collect evidence from the scene. The focus of the medical examiner investigator is to describe any evidence, or lack thereof, as well as trauma, environment and circumstances associated with the body of the decedent. They will write a report and provide me a copy of that report. I am provided with X-rays from the morgue staff and any other documentation before I begin my examination."

The medical examiner continued to explain the process of documenting and building a case file which ultimately results in a determination of cause and manner of death. The testimony lasted for almost two hours and went very smoothly. The doctor was very matter of fact, and there was no need for re-direct from the prosecution. "Thank you so much for your time and expertise Doctor. I am finished with this witness."

Richard took the next witness as well. She worked for the medical examiner's office as an investigator and was also a doctor, but not an M.D. When she sat in the witness box, Richard approached the stand after she was sworn in. "Ma'am, can you tell us your name, title, and position with the medical examiner's office?"

"My name is Dr. Helen Ward, and I am a Forensic Investigator and Forensic Anthropologist for the medical examiner's office."

"Will you please provide the court with your qualifications and educational background."

Dr. Ward rattled off her resume and curriculum vitae. Richard asked other qualifying questions before getting to the meat of his questioning. "Dr. Ward, do you know the defendant?"

"No, I do not."

"Have you ever seen the defendant before today?"

"Yes."

"In what capacity?"

"On the news," she answered.

"So, you have seen her, but have you spoken to her?"

"No, sir."

"Dr. Ward, in what capacity of your employment with the medical examiner's office did you handle this case?"

"I was called to the scene as an investigator."

"Did you prepare a report based on your observations of the body and its environment?"

"Yes."

"Would you briefly describe your observations of the victim to the court?"

Dr. Ward began describing how Mack was found and the condition of his remains. "He was far enough away from the road on the other side of the flood wall that he would not have been seen. His arms and legs were tethered to a long piece of metal that is consistent with construction material known as rebar. It appeared to have been hammered into the ground in a vertical manner." She then gave a little more information dealing with his body positioning.

"Did Mr. Parkins sustain any physical injuries?"

"Yes."

"Can you describe what you observed?"

Dr. Ward began to describe the injuries she observed, "Mr. Parkins sustained multiple fractures—"

"One moment Dr. Ward. My apologies for the interruption so soon, but without an X-ray, how are you able to discern someone has sustained such an injury?"

"There were obvious external abnormalities to some of the bones, which in my experience as an investigator and forensic anthropologist indicated trauma. In addition to the obvious trauma, I manipulated some of the bones and was able to note a shift, if you will, that was present in some areas that would not have that shift were the bones not fractured."

"Were there any other injuries other than the fractures?" he asked her.

"Yes. I observed what is consistent with sharp force trauma, inflicted by something with a sharp edge."

"So, a knife?"

"It could have been anything with a sharp edge, not just a knife."

"Dr. Ward, did you or the police crime scene unit find any weapons of any kind on the scene."

"No."

"Did you, at any point in the investigation, serve in the capacity of a forensic anthropologist?"

"Yes, I did."

"Can you explain what that entailed?"

"Once the remains were transported to the morgue, they are photographed and x-rayed to ascertain the extent of the injuries. I received previous digital images from Mr. Parkins' physicians that contained images of fractures he had sustained in the past. Once I received the images, I compared them to the images taken by our morgue staff. From there I was able to determine and verify the location of the more recent fractures.

"Thank you, Dr. Ward. I am finished with this witness."

CHAPTER 32

Penelope spoke up from her seat. "Dr. Ward, I only have a few questions for you." She stood up and walked towards the witness stand. "Based on your experience and knowledge, are you able to determine inflicted the injuries based on the location and type of fractures sustained to the victim?"

"No ma'am," she replied.

"Dr. Ward, are you able to discern how many people have inflicted the injuries?"

"Absolutely not."

"I just want to clarify, there is nothing in your experience and observations that indicates that my client, Mrs. Parker, was the person to inflict the injuries to Mack Parkins?"

"No ma'am. There is no way to tell who, how many, or what biological sex the person who inflicted the trauma is by using digital images or the naked eye."

"Thank you, Dr. Ward."

Richard could feel eyes staring at him from behind. He turned around briefly to see his boss talking to the president of the Board of Police Commissioners. The president was doing most of the talking, and his boss was getting an earful. The good news was, he wasn't the only person to see this happening. Ingrid also saw it, raising her eyebrows when Richard made eye contact with her. When Penelope finished her questioning, Richard stood up and said, "Your Honor, the People have no more witnesses at this time." As he sat back down, he caught Penelope looking at him with a puzzled look on her face. He could tell she knew something was going on, but she still didn't know what it was.

A recess was called for the remainder of the day. The judge said he did not want to start testimony that may run late into the day. He also had a meeting scheduled for early in the evening and could not be late. Richard watched the interaction between Kris and the same two women that left with her the previous day. He could also see her husband walking behind her, but their periodic interaction was not quite as intimate as what it was with the two women. The old Richard would have capitalized on that, but he wasn't going to do that. He could have used her husband's cheating to provide a motive for killing Mack. A woman wronged by all the men in her life, and she took it out on Mack first is what he would have done, but not this time.

Richard went to bed early and slept very well. As he was walking into the office to check emails; Ingrid was once again waiting for him. "Good morning, Ingrid. How did you sleep?" he asked.

"Not very well. I am extremely worried about you. What are you up to Richard?"

"Close the door. Actually, let's step outside in the fresh air." Once they got outside of the building, Richard started telling Ingrid his plan. As he was telling her, tears were streaming down her face. "I knew you would try to stop me, but now that I am at the point of no return, there is no way to do so."

"I really wish you would have said something sooner. I will be here for you when you need it, Richard. You have been my rock in this place, and I cannot ever repay you."

"You already have by making me the promise that you would leave the office after this trial is over. You must keep it now because you will be needed more at the next stop in your career."

Ingrid was still crying but was able to gather herself. "You really did think of everything, didn't you?" she said, referring to the promise he insisted she make.

"I did indeed. Now, let's go get some coffee and get this day started."

Penelope's list of witnesses included many of Kris's friends who were able to corroborate her whereabouts during the periods she was in St. Louis, as well as the time period when it was believed Mack was murdered. Richard did not rip any of them apart during his cross examination, and he only questioned one of them a little longer than the others pertaining to the timeline.

Ronnie was on the stand when he questioned her. "Mrs. Lowell."

"Detective Lowell," she corrected him.

"My most sincere apologies, Detective. You told Miss Clinton that you have known the defendant for quite some time, correct?"

"Yes, sir."

"How would you describe your relationship with Mrs. Parker?"

"Currently or our past relationship?"

"Both if you don't mind."

"Well, as I said before, we were in the St. Louis Police Academy together and worked closely together until she left the department. After that, we lost touch until last year."

"And how did you reconnect?"

"I worked on some committees with her older sister, Cat. I commented on something Cat had posted on a social media site, and we got in touch through the same platform."

"Is the current nature of your relationship different in any way than it was in the past?"

"Somewhat. I am much nicer than I was during our time at the academy. Our friendship is much closer than before. I guess we all grew up and learned the value of people who always have each other's backs. I know I have."

"Did you spend much time with Mrs. Parker when she was in town?"

"As much as we could between my work schedule and her visits with family and other friends. I know on one occasion she had an appointment with a doctor while she was visiting."

"Do you recall the day you both visited the police academy library."

"Yes sir."

"Can you tell me about that day?"

"We went to the library to look for a picture of one of the cadets who went through the academy."

"Who is the cadet you were looking for?"

"Shaen Finney."

"Why?"

"Because she wanted to match a face and name to the second person who raped her the same day Mack Parkins did."

"Allegedly," Richard corrected her.

"Sure," Ronnie replied.

"So, what you are saying is, she didn't actually know the name of the second person involved?"

"Not for a long time, but at one point she remembered the first name and the first letter of his last name."

"And when was she able to get the last name?"

"The day we went to the police academy library."

"Did Mrs. Parker view a photo line-up when she was filing charges?"

"Yes sir, she did."

"Do you know what the outcome of that viewing was?"

"Only from what Kris, Mrs. Parker told me."

"And what did she tell you?"

"She said half of the six pictures were not even close to the description she provided the police, and the other three she knew from the district or the academy."

"Thank you. So back to your visit to the library. Why did you go there instead of pulling photos from the officer files?"

Ronnie explained her reasoning for suggesting the library to Kris, including the fact that she did not need prying eyes on her. Ronnie worked in the Homicide Division, not Sex Crimes and she did not want the questions if she had taken Kris to her floor to look at personnel files. "Detective, are you saying you had to hide what you were doing?"

"Yes sir."

"Why?" Richard asked.

"Because the department was already trying to hide everything, and I was helping her try to expose Mack and who we now know was Shaen."

"But the statute of limitations had run out a long time ago. What did it matter?"

"I am not in her head, so I don't know why she would want to find out. Closure maybe?"

"Could be. Tell me, Detective, what did you do when you were finished at the academy library?"

"We went out and picked up some chocolate and lunch on the way back to my house."

"Did you work that night?"

"Yes sir."

"Were you with Mrs. Parker until you went to work?"

"No sir. I went into the house and went to sleep."

"Where did Mrs. Parker go?"

"She got a phone call and had to pick up a copy of the police report. She got it from the first civil litigation attorney she saw."

"Did you go back there with her?" Richard asked.

"No. I just told you I went into my house and slept."

"So, she could have gone anywhere at that point, and you would not have known any different?"

"Yes sir, she could have gone anywhere, and I would not have known."

"Thank you, Detective Lowell."

CHAPTER 33

The judge dismissed Ronnie from the stand, and Penelope called Derrick Hinton to the stand. He was also a graduate of the police academy and had been a former lover of Kris's. Penelope had gone into detail of the relationship with Derrick and at one point during the testimony, Ingrid stood up and objected for clarification of relevance. Penelope explained she was getting to it, but the court would need to let her do so. The judge overruled the objection allowing Penelope to continue. It did not take long before Penelope got to where Richard was thinking she was headed with her questioning. She asked Derrick to describe the incident that occurred, causing them to break up.

"Mrs. Parker was leaving my house for work, and I had to tell her I had gotten married the weekend before."

"How did she take that news?"

"Not well. She was almost out the door when I told her. I think my approach at telling her could have been much better."

"Did she say anything to you, or do something to you?" Penelope asked.

"Yes," Derrick replied.

"Which is it?"

"She said and did something. When I told her I had gotten married she said, 'That is awfully brave for you to say that when I have my gun on my hip, and you are 10 feet away from yours.'"

"Did she draw her weapon?"

"No, ma'am."

"Were you in fear for your life?"

"Not at any point during the exchange."

"Why not?"

"Because it is not like her to do something like that. Kris is a very strong woman, and she knows how to handle setbacks. She was speaking out of a place of hurt and disappointment."

"Thank you, Special Agent Hinton. Your witness Counselor."

Richard stood up and approached the witness stand. "Thank you for being here, Special Agent Hinton. How long were you and Mrs. Parker seeing each other?"

"A couple of years."

"Were you in an intimate relationship from the start, or did it develop over time?"

"Our friendship started in the academy but once she graduated, we lost touch until we worked a Fourth of July fair together. We made plans to meet for dinner one night and from then on it was an intimate relationship."

"Mr. Hinton, did you ever develop stronger feelings for Mrs. Parker?"

"I did, but I never told her."

"Did she develop stronger feelings for you?"

"I don't know."

"Why did you never tell her of the feelings you had for her?"

"Because she told me she did not want any committed relationship, at least not the kind that leads to marriage. At the time I broke things off with her, I figured it would be easier on me to already be married and be nonchalant about it."

"Did you see Mrs. Parker after you were married?"

"I did."

"In what capacity?"

"I went to her apartment after getting off shift early one morning."

"Were you not afraid? She did all but threaten to kill you the last time you saw her."

"I was never afraid of Mrs. Parker at any point in our relationship. I was not afraid the day she left my house, and I was not afraid to see her the morning I showed up at her apartment."

"What happened that next time you saw her?"

"We talked into the early hours of the morning after making love one more time."

"How did that departure go?"

"Much better than the previous one, although we both cried. I think we knew it was the last time we would ever see each other again."

"Thank you, Agent Hinton. One more question. When did you last speak with Mrs. Parker?"

"I think it was while she was in the process of dealing with the courts about the rape. She left a message on my desk phone asking me to call her from a private line. That is when she told me about Mack and another officer raping her."

"Allegedly raping her," Richard corrected.

"Sure. Allegedly. Anyway, she described the other officer to me, and I remembered him but only that his first name was Shaen and his last name started with an F."

"How well did you know Mack Parkins?"

"Just in passing and small talk at the station."

"How well did you know Detective Finney?"

Derrick got a scowl on his face, "I was made to partner up with Shaen. We all worked the same shift."

"Did you hang out with them after work?"

"Not if I could help it," Derrick replied.

"Why is that?"

"Because they were all corrupt as hell, and I did not want to be a part of that."

"Corrupt how?"

"I was invited to go to a party after work one evening, so I went, and stayed until the extra party favors were being distributed to the women."

"Do you know what they were being given?"

"No, but I can only assume it was some sort of date rape drug. Mack was known for that kind of activity."

"Can you explain what you mean by 'that kind of activity'?"

"He had a reputation for drugging women and raping them."

"Who else was at the party?"

Derrick started to name off a list of officers who were at the party, some of which were sitting in the gallery, as well as the ensuing crimes that followed. "…and Shaen Finney was there as well."

"Did you ever report these activities to the higher ups in the department?" Richard asked.

"Who was I going to tell? Mack's father was Captain down at headquarters. Mack was untouchable. My life would have been made into a living hell. I kept my head down and left the department as soon as I could, just like anyone else who had a conscience and a soul."

"Okay. I want to go back to the day Mrs. Parker told you about the alleged rape that happened."

"Okay," Derrick replied.

"What was your reaction when she told you about the incident?"

"I was pissed, and I was hurting for my friend, for the woman who had a piece of my heart, even now."

"What, if anything, did you say to Mrs. Parker?"

"I told her how sorry I was that it had happened and that I wished there was something I could do for her. The sad part is, I was not surprised by Mack's actions, but I was at Shaen's."

"Why is Shaen's alleged involvement more surprising to you?"

"Well," Derrick explained, "At the time Mack and Shaen raped –"

"Allegedly," Richard reminded him.

"Right, sorry. At the time they ALLEGEDLY raped Kris, he was nothing more than a whiny little bitch."

This time the judge spoke up. "Son, please watch your language in my courtroom." Richard was getting a kick out of it, and he winked at Derrick, egging him on.

"My apologies, Your Honor. I should not have called him that. It is an insult to female dogs."

Richard watched Derrick stare directly at Shaen, "What I meant to say, is that Shaen was a follower, a coward, and a pussy."

CHAPTER 34

Now Richard turned his gaze toward Shaen, and the look on his face as Derrick spoke was one that could not be described. This was one hell of a show, and he was enjoying every second of it. Penelope had not objected to any of Richard's cross-examination. All she could see was him sabotaging this case, and she was content to let him do so. "AGENT HINTON!" the judge yelled. "This will be the last time I ask you to curb your language. Next time you will be in jail, with your one phone call being to your supervisor, explaining why you are being charged with contempt of court. Do I make myself clear?"

"Sorry, Your Honor, I chose to use the shortened version of pusillanimous, which means to show a lack of courage or determination," Derrick said with a smile.

Richard let Derrick finish answering the question. Derrick described Shaen as a person who did not know how to take the reins and that he seemed like someone who would go to Internal Affairs. "Knowing what I know about him, the only way he would have ALLEGEDLY done such a despicable act, was if someone told him he had to. He surely was not smart enough to have orchestrated or help plan that sort of thing."

"Thank you. How did your conversation with Mrs. Parker end?"

"We said goodbye, and that was it. I got a couple of emails from time to time, including when she found Shaen's full name."

"So, nothing else was said?"

"No."

"Are you sure?" Richard asked, already knowing the answer.

"I may have mentioned something about taking a road trip soon."

"Thank you, Agent Hinton, I am finished with this witness."

The judge excused Derrick from the witness stand, and as Richard approached his table, his boss leaned forward and through a clenched jaw and red face, said to him, "You may have well just given this case to them on a silver platter." And stormed out of the courtroom. The judge called a recess for lunch. He looked at Ingrid and asked if she wanted to do the rest of the questioning. "Chances are I am going to be pulled as lead at lunch. You know what to do." He told her. Up to this point, they had been taking turns questioning and cross-examining witnesses. They sat at lunch and talked strategy.

The boss caught him walking to the sidewalk, informing him he was no longer lead counsel, and appointed Ingrid to the lead position. "Richard, this is going to be your last case. You mark my words," his boss said to him.

"Oh, I believe you sir. I will even go so far as to say that I agree with you," Richard replied.

After lunch, Penelope's next witness was Adrienne Shiffer. She provided her credentials and the length of time she had been treating Kris. She spoke of Kris's diagnoses and the treatment plan she was working on with her. Penelope did not ask questions that would have required details of their sessions because she already knew Adrienne did not keep detailed notes. Ingrid stood up and began her cross. "Miss Shiffer, you told Miss Clinton that you have been treating Mrs. Parker off and on since 2009, is that correct?"

"Yes, that is correct."

"Why off and on?"

"When I first started treating Kris, I was working for a military organization that provided mental health care for military members and their dependents. They were solution focused with their treatment so they limited the number of sessions for the clients

"Did Mrs. Parker attend all of her sessions?"

"Yes, and I fought for her to receive more."

"Why would you do that?"

"As I said earlier, Mrs. Parker was initially diagnosed with Post Traumatic Stress Disorder and was later changed to a diagnosis of Generalized Anxiety Disorder." Adrienne began to explain what the diagnoses criteria were according to the DSM-IV. "Right before our sessions ended, she discovered her husband had been cheating on her, and her anxiety only got worse."

"Did she disclose to you that she had been raped by two of her co-workers from the police department at that time?"

"No, she did not."

"What happened after your sessions ended, or I should say, when you reached the limit of sessions?"

"About six months later, I heard from her husband, Tony, who said he and Kris were engaged in a verbal argument when she suddenly went catatonic. He was extremely concerned for her and asked me to give her a call."

"What was the outcome of that call?"

"I provided her the name and number of a colleague who could see her near the campus she was attending classes at."

"And did she see this person?"

"Yes, and then came back to me for treatment when that therapist closed her practice."

"Is this when she disclosed the rape to you?"

"She never officially disclosed to me. It was her other therapist as well as a second one she saw in conjunction for a specialized kind of cognitive therapy."

"What kind of specialized therapy?"

"It is referred to as EMDR, which stands for Eye Movement Desensitization and Reprocessing. The goal is for the person receiving the therapy be able to discuss it in a way that separates the emotions and physical reactions from the trauma, as well as helping them recall information, since they are in a more grounded position."

"So, hypnosis?"

"No ma'am. We do not hypnotize people."

"Miss Shiffer, can you explain how that works then?"

"The patient is taught to focus on an object or light with their eyes as it moves back and forth, like following a tennis match volley. During this process, the client is describing their trauma and learning how to not react physically or emotionally because they are focused on the object or light. If done correctly, the client will also report any new thoughts about the trauma.

Ingrid waited for her to finish describing the process of EMDR, "Miss Shiffer, I recall when you provided your qualifications, you stated that you are EMDR certified as well, is that correct?"

"Yes. That is correct," Adrienne replied.

"Did you treat Mrs. Parker with EMDR therapy?"

"Yes. We would do EMDR in conjunction with Cognitive Behavioral Therapy."

"What is Cognitive Behavioral Therapy?" Ingrid asked.

"Simply put, it is talking therapy. I would alternate what we did at each session, but I was fluid with my treatment. It would always depend on what Kris was feeling and needed at the time of the session."

"At any time during her therapy, did you ever suggest to Mrs. Parker the idea that she had been raped?"

"Never."

"Were you able to plant memories of an incident that never happened?"

Adrienne was quite offended by the mere thought of someone doing this to a client, "Absolutely NOT! I let my clients talk, and I listen until I think I need to ask probative questions. It helps them to expand on what they are expressing to me already. And please, do not forget, I was not the person she originally disclosed the rape to."

"That's right. She told the person you sent her to, Elaine Hutchens, correct?"

"That is correct."

"How well would you say you know Mrs. Parker?"

"After treating her for as long as I have been, I would say quite well."

"Would you characterize your relationship as being friends?"

"No, and somewhat yes," Adrienne answered.

"How can it be both?"

"No, because it is unethical to be friends with clients, but the caveat to that is that if she were not my client, and I were to have met her in some other circumstances, we would more than likely be friends."

"Just friends?"

"Yes. Just friends?"

"Okay. As her therapist, would you do anything for Mrs. Parker?"

"Anything within reason and the law, yes. I will never jeopardize my license for anyone."

"You said within reason and the law as her therapist. What about as her friend?"

"We aren't friends. She is my client."

Ingrid also saw the exchange between the two when Adrienne had been calming Mrs. Parker. "Let's say that you were friends, maybe even more, would you do anything for Mrs. Parker?"

"I suppose I would."

"Even kill for her?" Ingrid asked.

"No," Adrienne said emphatically.

"Okay, thank you for your time, Miss Schiffer." She walked away from the stand, studying the jury. One more seed of doubt planted. She sure hoped Richard knew what he was doing, because the boss was not looking happy with her either.

CHAPTER 35

Penelope called Elaine Hutchens to the stand, asking many of the same questions. There were some questions pertaining to the destruction of Kris's therapy notes, which apparently had not actually been destroyed. Elaine put the originals in a safe place and made copies.

"Why did you destroy them?" Penelope asked.

"I was being threatened if I didn't."

"Threatened by whom and what specific threats were made?"

"Mack Parkins was threatening to ruin my career and hurt my mother physically. I made him think I destroyed them and moved away where he could not find me or my mother." "Did it work?"

"For a while, then I got a note that said, 'I found you anyway.'" Elain replied.

"What did you do after that?"

"Nothing. I didn't tell anyone, and I just let it go."

"Did it finally stop?"

"Yes."

"When it was all happening, how did you feel? Sorry, now I sound like a therapist." Penelope said with a slight smile. A few giggles came from the gallery and jury box.

"I was extremely angry. Extremely angry and really scared," Elaine told her.

"Why were you scared Miss Hutchens?

"I was scared for the safety of my mom."

"Would you do anything to protect her?"

"Absolutely."

"Miss Hutchens, would you kill for your mother?"

Elaine knew this question was coming. It was being done with every witness being called on Kris's behalf, and it was being done to plant doubt in the minds of the jury. "Under certain circumstances, yes."

"Thank you. I am finished with this witness."

"Your honor, the people have no further questions for this witness." The boss and officers sitting in the gallery were fuming. Penelope and Kris were in a private conversation. The judge was repeatedly asking for her to call her next witness, which was Kris. At that point, Richard and Ingrid watched Ronnie rush out of the courtroom and three other detectives followed, including Terry and Derrick.

A smile spread across Richard's face because he knew why they had left, that is, except Ronnie. He was not sure what she had to do with any of this. Ronnie came back in with a woman in tow. When Penelope saw her, she requested to change her witness from Kris to the woman. The judge agreed but asked Ingrid if there were any objections to the witness testifying since she was not on the witness list. Normally, there would have been, but Ingrid knew why she was not to object. The woman testified to an incident that occurred at hotel with her then fiancé, now her husband. She testified to the fact that Shaen sexually assaulted her and told her the department would not file charges against them if she would have sexual intercourse with him.

"Why did you never report it?" Penelope asked.

"I told my probation officer."

"What was his or her response?"

"She said I should have reported it too."

"And why didn't you?"

"Because he threatened me and my husband with additional charges if we said anything."

"I am so sorry this happened. How did you react at the time?"

"Well, I just complied by keeping my mouth shut, but I was so angry."

"And when you were told about this alleged incident with Mrs. Parker, how did you feel?"

"Sick to my stomach, angry, and sad for Mrs. Parker."

"Do you know Mrs. Parker?"

"No."

"Did you know Mack Parkins?"

"No, but he deserved what he got because the only thing he trained Detective Finney in is how to get away with this kind of stuff."

"Thank you. I am finished with this witness."

Ingrid stood up, "We have nothing for this witness at this time, Your Honor." More angry faces from their side of the gallery.

A recess was called for lunch before Kris testified. The boss came up to Ingrid and Richard when everyone filed out of the courtroom. "You will BOTH be packing your shit up when this is over."

Richard looked over at Ingrid and laughed. "We have already started," he responded.

"Do you know the shit I am getting from the police department? They have cut off my funds and are threatening me. You better damn well have something big planned to turn this around."

Richard patted his boss's arm, "No worries boss, I do."

CHAPTER 36

After lunch, Penelope called Kris to the stand, and jumped in with both feet, asking Kris, "Did you kill Mack Parkins?"

"Absolutely not."

"Is there any reason you would want Mack dead Mrs. Parker?"

"No."

Penelope then read a portion of Kris's police report that had been filed for the alleged rape. "Given what was done to you, you can honestly say you wouldn't want to see Mack Parkins dead or even Shaen Finney dead?"

Kris answered confidently, "Yes, I can honestly say that I did not want to see them dead. They had done enough to me already, there is no way I was going to jail for doing something to them."

"Mrs. Parker, how many times did you visit St. Louis when you were filing charges and dealing with the courts?"

"At least three times? Maybe four? I had already planned the visits for family events and arranged my visits to the police department and lawyers around those visits. All the dealings with the police department happened on the same visit. I was made aware of the statute of limitations not long after I filed the report."

"Did you come back home specifically to see the civil attorneys?"

"Just the first one. The second set of attorneys I saw was during another family event visit, and I scheduled the appointment for when I had free time."

Penelope continued her questioning, asking for times of her appointments, establishing an alibi for each visit, specifically for when Mack was last heard from alive. "Mrs. Parker, I know I have asked you a lot of personal questions, but would you indulge me one more time and provide me with your height, weight and a brief medical history."

"I am 5'3", 175 pounds, and what kind of medical history are you looking for?"

"Do you have any medical conditions that would prevent you from doing anything physical or exerting yourself?"

"Well, I was born three months early and I have lung issues once in a while. I have seasonal asthma and depending on the situation, I am prone to asthma attacks."

"Can you give me an example?"

"Well, if it is too hot and humid out and I am doing something outside that is strenuous, such as running, I start coughing and it turns into an asthma attack."

"Thank you."

Smart move Richard thought. He leaned over and said something about it to Ingrid, and she nodded in agreement.

"Mrs. Parker, do you own any weapons that you travel with when you come to St. Louis?"

"Not this time," she told Penelope.

This prompted a giggle from quite a few people in the courtroom. "Prior to this visit, did you travel with any kind of weapon?"

"Yes."

"What kind of weapon?"

"I would bring my old nightstick from the department with me."

"Could you describe the nightstick?"

"It is made of solid hickory and has two brass caps on the end. They are screwed into place, and it was handmade by an officer in the department."

Penelope picked up a stick matching the description Kris just provided. "Mrs. Parker, is this your nightstick?"

"It looks like it. I would need to see the handle end of it. My old DSN, I'm sorry, department service number, is stamped on the bottom of the brass cap."

"What was your DSN?"

"4302."

Penelope approached Kris, showing her the end of the stick, with the numbers 4302 stamped on the end of the cap. "I will ask again, is this your nightstick?"

"It appears so."

"Mrs. Parker, when was the last time you saw this nightstick?"

"I had not seen it since the day I arrived in St. Louis and unpacked my car."

"Did you unpack it the same day?"

"Yes, but I also put it back in there when I would go to the city."

"Did you take it with you when you went to see the second set of civil attorneys?"

"Yes ma'am."

"Where did you keep it?"

"In the trunk area of my car."

"When did you know it was missing?"

"The same day Detectives Lowell and Chaney showed up at my parents' house to tell me about Mack. We were looking for it all over the house and my car."

"Thank you, Mrs. Parker. Nothing further, your witness counselor," Penelope said to Ingrid.

CHAPTER 37

Ingrid looked at Richard and he nodded, letting her know he had faith in her to finish the case. "Mrs. Parker, thank you for taking the stand. Not many defendants would do that in a situation like this. All of these officers are glaring at you … it's a good thing they don't have daggers coming out of their eyes. Why do you think they are so angry with you?"

"Seriously? Have you been here this entire trial?"

"Humor me, please," Ingrid winked at Kris. Kris looked at Ingrid with a shocked look on her face. While she did not overtly respond to the wink, Ingrid could tell Kris was stunned. "I am not trying to sound condescending. Why are all of these cops and other members of the department so angry with you?" "Because they think I killed Mack Parkins."

"And did you kill Mack Parkins?"

"No. I did not."

"If you did not kill him, I mean, according to you, he allegedly raped you, why WOULD'NT you kill him? I'm sorry, I got off topic. If you didn't kill him, who else would want him dead? You had the best motive."

"I would guess that previous victims, family, friends … his WIFE, all may have wanted him dead. I surely did not corner the market on that sentiment," Kris answered.

"Fair enough. The question is, why would anyone frame you?"

"Ma'am, with all due respect, did you hit your head? I am beginning to think we are not in the same room."

"I know these are not the best questions, but they are necessary," Ingrid told her. "So, I ask again, why would anyone frame you? Some of the people who could be suspects are your family. Why would they frame you?"

"My family? They wouldn't. Members of the police department?

Because they want me to pay for attempting to spoil the reputation of such a wonderful' guy. I am the most logical because I am now the scorned lover with a grudge."

"How were you spoiling the reputation of Mack Parkins?"

"By filing a police report for the rape, he and Shaen carried out when I was a police officer."

"And Mack Parkins was the accused?"

"At the time, yes, but only because I did not know Shaen's full name."

"Did you, or do you now, have any thoughts on how the investigation was handled?"

"Yes. I don't think it was handled at all."

"Mrs. Parker, can you explain what you mean by that?"

"I think they swept it under the rug before it even arrived in your office. It was a half-assed investigation. I think they knew it would go nowhere, that the statute of limitations was up, and they fed me shit, all the while telling me it was sugar."

Kris's remark about shit and sugar got a few snickers from the courtroom, including from Richard. The judge, however, did not find it funny. "Mrs. Parker, could you please limit the language?"

"I am sorry Your Honor. I will not let it happen again."

"By that statement, are you implying that you think they are corrupt?"

"Who, the department?" Kris asked.

"Sure, we can start there," she smiled at Kris.

"Hell, yes, they are. They were from the time I started and long before that. My own training officer was as dirty as they get. I almost got fired before I was off probation because I would not fabricate evidence and plant things on people for a notch in my belt. I watched them take money from people, plant drugs, make charges go way, tickets disappear, and extort sexual favors from women in exchange for not arresting them, whether the charge was legitimate or made up."

"Anyone else you think is corrupt?"

"Maybe not everyone, but your office and some of the judges."

"What makes you think that Mrs. Parker?"

"Because of the way both cases have been handled. One has been brushed under the rug and forgotten and one rushed to conclusions. I am the only person anyone ever looked at for killing Mack."

"Did you hate Mack Parkins?"

"At first, when I started to remember the rape and when I wasn't able to file charges, yes."

"Did you want him dead?"

"No. As I said before, neither of them was worth going to jail for."

"Mrs. Parker, when did you remember Shaen's name and connect him with having been the other person involved in your alleged rape?"

"It all came together at different times. I remembered his first name while sitting with my friend Kate and confirmed it with Agent Hinton when I spoke with him. I really knew when Detective Lowell and I went to the police academy library."

"Aren't the names of the cadets on the back of the photos?"

"Yes."

"And you used the class pictures as a reference, correct?"

"Yes, that is correct."

"So, it would have been easy to look on the back to find his name and look at the picture whether you remembered his face or not."

"I guess if you wanted to lie about it just because you wanted to see someone get in trouble for something they didn't do, sure." Kris looked at the officers gathered in the room who had been glaring at her from day one. "And did you?"

"Did I what?"

"Want to see someone get in trouble for something they didn't do?"

"No, I wanted them both to be punished for what they DID do! I wanted them to go to prison not to be killed."

"You are not very ambitious are you Mrs. Parker?"

"Excuse me?!" Kris yelled. At the same time, Penelope sprung out of her chair and the judge called all the attorneys for a sidebar.

"Counselor, either start asking appropriate questions and refrain from making statements and being argumentative with the witness or end the questioning."

"Yes, Your Honor. My apologies," Ingrid said.

"Don't apologize to me, apologize to your witness," the judge instructed.

"Mrs. Parker, I am sincerely sorry for my remark. I only meant that if they had done that to me, I would have asked God for BOTH outcomes."

The judge looked at Ingrid, "Counselor, you are very close to crossing a line."

"Yes, Your Honor. Mrs. Parker let's go back to when you said you did not remember Shaen's name until later. Did you ever contact or receive any contact from either of the men?"

"No, I did not."

"Mrs. Parker, do you hate men?"

"No, I do not."

Penelope stood, raising an objection. Ingrid argued her point, "Your Honor, it's a valid question. If she hates men, it could prove motive."

"Point made Counselor," the judge said. He mumbled under his breath, "What in the hell is going on?"

CHAPTER 38

When Ingrid turned around, Richard was handing something to an intern. A short time later, the intern handed something to Ronnie out in the hallway. Ronnie opened it and went to her seat right behind Penelope. Richard saw Ronnie hand the paper to Penelope who read it and looked at him with a puzzled face. At the same time, John, Penelope's investigator, came into the courtroom, handing a large envelope to Penelope. She asked for a 10-minute recess. The judge told Kris to sit back with Penelope. Richard left the court room to use the men's room. On his way out, he nodded at Derrick and Terry. At the other end of the hall was his boss, most of the Board of Police Commissioners and Chiefs of Police and Chiefs of Police.

"Richard—"

Richard cut the Chief of Police off before a threat could be made. "Don't worry Chief, my colleague and I have this handled." They stepped back into the courtroom, the judge returned, and Kris was directed back to the witness stand.

"Mrs. Parker, I have nothing further for you," Ingrid said. "Thank you for your time."

Everyone sitting on the side of the prosecution was befuddled. *Why had Kris not been torn apart? What was going on?* some thought.

After reading the note from Richard, Penelope stood up and addressed the judge, "Your Honor, in light of some new information I received, I would like to recall Detective Finney to the stand." The judge asked, "As a witness for the defense or prosecution?"

"For the defense your honor, although I will have to reference his previous testimony."

"Do The People have any objections?"

Ingrid stood up, "No, Your Honor."

"Counselor, you may proceed," the judge told her.

Shaen was called back to the witness stand and sworn back in. As he was walking to the stand, Ingrid and Richard both saw Kris's dark-haired friend put a hand on her shoulder.

"Detective Finney, I recalled you because I wanted to clarify some of your answers from your previous testimony."

"Okay," he said, the smirk still missing from his face.

"You stated earlier that you had a sexual encounter with Mrs. Parker, is that correct?'

"Yes."

"And you also stated it was purely consensual, in fact it was her idea even AFTER she had somewhat sobered up?"

"That is also correct."

"So, tell me then Detective, why would Mack have been blackmailing you?"

"What?"

"I am sure you heard me, but I will repeat the question. Why would Mack Parkins have been blackmailing you?"

Shaen hung his head and lifted it back up knowing he'd been outed. "He said if I didn't help him sabotage Kris's case, he would tell them who else was there that day and also expose the affair I had been having."

"Well, the current affair I get, but if the sex was consensual, why would it matter if your name was given?"

"I didn't want my wife to find out."

"You didn't want her to find out that you raped someone? I wouldn't want that known either."

"Yes, I mean no. I didn't want her to know I cheated on her before we were even married."

"So, to avoid your name being exposed, you let him blackmail you?"

"Yes."

"What was Mack Parkins like Detective Finney? You painted him as a hero, yet this same person was blackmailing you. So, tell me. What do you really think of him?"

"I said before, he was a good guy and I liked working with him."

"Did he orchestrate the rape of Mrs. Parker?"

"Yes."

"When you started meeting Mack to get your "debt" paid off, why, when you had him tied up, did you use a nightstick, Mrs. Parker's nightstick to be exact, to inflict bodily injury to a man you say was a "good guy"?

"I didn't do that."

"Oh, but you did. Your Honor, I would like to submit evidence that refutes Detective Finney's statement." Penelope plugged in a video tape that clearly shows Mack and Shaen together behind the flood wall, arguing. She paused the tape. "Would you like to tell me the rest of what is on that video, or should I keep playing it for the jury?"

"It is me arguing with Mack. So what?" Shaen said nonchalantly.

"Suit yourself," Penelope said as she raised her hand to restart the video.

"FINE!" he yelled. "I will tell you what happened." Shaen started his story. "After I finished some errands – "

"What did you do on the errands?" she asked.

"I went to the bank, and then I went to the store."

"The grocery store?"

"No, the hardware store."

"What did you buy?"

"Cut pieces of rebar, tape, and rope."

"Then what?" Penelope asked.

"Then I went down behind the flood wall and measured out an area to put the rebar in. I had a bag of quick setting concrete in my trunk from a home project I had worked on. A few hours later, I called Mack and told him where to meet me."

"Did he not question why you wanted to meet after telling him you wouldn't?"

"He did, and then I told him I had changed my mind."

"Please continue Detective."

"After I got everything set up, I moved my car so he would not see the rebar. I sat in my car and waited for him. The moment he arrived; he started dogging me just like he did when we worked together. I had had it with his abuse, so when he turned to walk away, I hit him with a taser until he fell to the ground. I pulled the trigger so much, I made him pass out, but that was fine, because I needed him subdued."

"Did he ever come to?"

"Yes," Shaen answered.

"How was he when he woke up?"

"To say he was angry would be putting it mildly. I had to drag him to the spot where the rebar had been set up, and he had some cuts and scrapes on his chest. It was hot out too, so when his sweat ran into the cuts and scrapes, it stung."

"Is that all?"

"No. I undressed him completely before securing him to the rebar posts."

"Did you further physically assault Mack?"

"Yes."

"What did you do to him Detective?"

"I grabbed Mrs. Parker's nightstick from my car, and –"

"Wait, YOU took the nightstick?"

"Yes," Shaen answered.

"How did you manage that?"

"When she went to the attorney's office downtown, I had been following her and after she went in, I broke into her car to get it."

"What else did you do to Mack Parkins, Detective?"

"I struck him a few times with the nightstick."

"Hard?"

"Not extremely hard, but it inflicted pain."

"It also inflicted some fractures."

"Okay," Shaen replied with no ounce of concern in his voice.

"When you were done hitting him, then what did you do?"

"I left him there."

"Well, you did, but not before doing something else to him. I will forward the video so everyone can see if you don't want to say out loud what you did."

Shaen sat there just looking at Penelope. "I just left him where he was."

"Okay," she responded as she lifted her hand up again.

"FINE! I shoved the nightstick in him."

"You sodomized him."

"Yes, but I did not kill him. He was alive when I left."

"Oh, I know that because that is also on the video. Would you like to know what else is there?"

Shaen was nervous at this point because he had no clue what else could possibly be on that video tape. Penelope forwarded the recording until Shaen was seen driving away. The recording is aimed at Mack at this point, and it is moving closer to him. Finally, the person holding the camera comes into view because the person filming put the camera down.

CHAPTER 39

The video continued on the screen, and it showed Richard inflicting blow after blow using the nightstick he painfully removed from Mack's anus. Like Shaen, he was smart enough to wear gloves. Mack was screaming in pain, asking "Why?"

Penelope paused the tape. At that moment, officers and federal agents appeared in the courtroom, standing in various spots along the front and rear exits. Penelope turned and looked at Richard, and he nodded at her.

Penelope turned to the judge and said, "Your Honor, at this time I would like to have the charges against my client dropped and her record to reflect she was never even arrested. In addition to this tape, there are other documents that have been placed in my possession that will prove Richard McCullen killed Mack Parkins and framed my client."

The judge hung his head, "What does the State say?"

With tears streaming down her face, Ingrid spoke up, "We have no objections Your Honor. Your Honor, The State would also like to formally charge Richard McCullen for the assault and murder of Mack Parkins."

"Anything further, Counselor?"

"Yes, Your Honor," she was still trying to do her best to compose herself. She had been devastated when Richard told her he was going to turn evidence on everyone involved in the corruption between their office and the police department. "The State of Missouri would also like to formally charge Detective Shaen Finney with tampering with evidence, tampering with witnesses, perjury, and sodomy in the first degree."

The judge picked up his gavel to end the case, but Ingrid wasn't finished. "Your Honor, I would also like to charge the following members of the St. Louis Police Department for the following crimes ..." She listed them all, and one by one they were escorted out of the courtroom by officers and agents. "Lastly Your Honor," at which time she turned to a different judge who entered the courtroom unbeknownst to the sitting judge, "The State would like to formally charge The Honorable Judge Adam W. Vilipend for the following charges …"

"Young lady, you have no proof I have had contact with anyone about this case, let alone any jury members."

"I am sorry sir, but I do have proof. I learned from my predecessor to record things I think are important. After the first time I saw you talking to detectives, I approached them with Mr. McCullen, and they made a deal with this office. Your bribery and extortion are all on record." Federal agents, one of which was Derrick, took the judge into custody. As the new judge dismissed all charges and agreed to have Kris's record wiped clean, he told his bailiff to take Richard into custody.

"Wait," Richard said. "Please let me explain all of this to Mrs. Parker."

Ingrid spoke up, "Richard, you really shouldn't say anything until your trial."

"I am not going to a trial. I am going to request immediate sentencing."

Despite not playing football, Mack continued to work out. He managed to keep to himself the rest of the year and picked his grades up enough to graduate and go to a decent college. While he was away at college; he felt a little freer from the pressures he felt at home and in Texas.

Mack was built very nicely. When he wasn't in class, he was at the gym or running. He joined a fraternity and learned very quickly what he had to do to prove himself there. He did not get hazed, at least not all the time, and when he did it was normal for new fraternity members to be hazed.

The initiation was a cake walk compared to what he dealt with in high school. Sometimes, the games the new people had to play involved the sister sorority and there was more than a couple of girls interested in Mack. 'Of course, they want me, he thought. What's not to want?'

The problem for Mack was, if he even considered it to be a problem at this point, that he did not want the girls. He was not interested in being physical with them, but he did, to prove to himself he wasn't really feeling what he was when he was around some of the guys at the fraternity house.

When the initiation events involved some of the more senior members of the fraternity, Mack was much more comfortable. He figured out a couple of the guys were into him too. Again, he thought, Why wouldn't they? Just look at me. I am not some dumb jock, but I am nice to look at. They can keep admiring me. Mack stopped playing sports altogether. He wanted nothing more to do with that community.

He was asked to play college ball, but he refused, much to his father's dismay. He had, however, decided to go into law enforcement, like his dad. He was going to major in criminal justice and apply for the department after graduation. He also didn't date one girl exclusively, but nobody turned him down either. Even if they refused his advances, he still ended up with them. "No" was not a word Mack accepted, especially from a girl.

Mack no longer had access to the Ketamine as freely as he did in high school, but he didn't really need it. The parties flowed with alcohol and some of the girls who attended would get black out drunk, so they were the easiest for him to be with physically. He was only a freshman, but his confidence in himself grew leaps and bounds.

One night, after a big rivalry game, their frat house hosted the big party for the season. In walked a group of cheerleaders, one of them already on her way to becoming too drunk. She was pretty in an ordinary way, but it seemed to be what the guys liked. As he watched her, one of the male cheerleaders noticed and watched Mack watching her and said, "Good luck, man. She doesn't pay any guys any sort of attention."

Mack said exactly what he was thinking, "Maybe because none of them are as good-looking as I am."

"Well, aren't you full of yourself."

"I mean, you are nice looking and all, but you aren't good enough for her."

"Oh. And you are?" the guy asked Mack.

"Of course, in fact, I am TOO good for her."

"Look, all I am saying is she is hyper focused on school. She is a cheerleader because it is part of what is paying for school. I am honestly very surprised she is here tonight. One of her friends talked her into coming. Don't be surprised if she blows you off."

"Well," Mack said, "You are right about the blowing part."

The guy started laughing hard at this point which made Mack angry. "Oh sure, like THAT is going to happen."

Mack looked at the cheerleader and said, "Tell you what, I will have her in my room in the next hour, and when I do, just to prove to you I won't be told 'no' by her, you can join in on the fun."

The guy took a swig of his drink, stuck his hand out and said, "Deal!"

Forty-five minutes later, Mack and the girl were walking toward his room. He leaned in as he passed the male cheerleader and said, "Give me a few minutes, and then come in. The door will be unlocked." Mack pointed down the hall, told him which room was his and kept walking, holding the girl up because she was having difficulty doing it on her own.

"My legs are just so tired and weak," she said to Mack. "Maybe I should have someone take me home."

"Don't make your friends leave," Mack said. "They are having a good time. You can lay on my bed and rest for a while. I will let you know when they are leaving."

"I don't think that is a good idea."

"Trust me," he told her, it's a GREAT idea."

Mack helped her to bed and took her shoes off. "Let's get you more comfortable."

After a few minutes, the male cheerleader came in the room. The girl was lying on the bed, now Naked, and under the covers—the room spinning.

The next morning the girl woke up in her dorm room with a massive headache and did not remember what happened after getting to the frat house. Her roommate came in the door from the showers and said, "I am glad to see you are still alive. I was beginning to worry."

"I have a horrible headache."

"*I am surprised that is all you have.*"

"*What do you mean? the girl asked.*"

"*You were up in the room with the one frat guy and the male cheerleader for a while. They are the ones who brought you home.*"

She slowly sat up as she was saying, "I don't remember anything. Why can I not remember?"

"*I don't know. How much did you have to drink?*"

The girl thought for a minute. "I only had the one drink at the party, but I had a few before that but just one there."

"*Maybe that was the one that put you over the top.*"

"*I guess. I have never been drunk before, so maybe that is the issue.*"

"*Do you remember anything at all?" her roommate asked.*

"*No. Well, yes. I remember the room spinning and the frat guy taking me to his room to rest.*

After that, everything is a blur," Julia said as she slowly stood up. When she did, it was her roommate that noticed the stain on her sheets.

"*Oh. My. God. What happened to you?*"

"*What are you talking about?*"

The other girl pointed to the bed, pointing out the blood stain.

CHAPTER 40

Kris and Penelope both approached him, and he explained what happened between Mack and his daughter, Julia, when she was in college. After years of Mack stalking and tormenting her, she killed herself. Mack had never been charged for any of it. When he saw everything coming across his desk, he knew this would be his only opportunity to do what needed to be done. It was a good thing that police officers have such big egos because if they didn't, he may not have overheard much of the information from other officers. One of the people he overheard was an officer Shaen worked with. Richard approached him about what he had overheard. The officer told Richard that Shaen was in the bar one night bragging about what he and Mack had done so long ago, and that Kris hadn't remembered Shaen by name, so he was in the clear. "That apparently was when Mack started to blackmail him," Richard told Kris.

"I started following Shaen and Mack, and I happened to follow Mack that day. I started to video the moment I saw the two of them together. When I saw Mack lying there, alive, I became so enraged, I killed him. He was left alive, to get away with something else. I had no plans of allowing that to happen. My Julia killed herself because of that man. He had to be stopped."

Richard looked at Kris, "Young lady, I am so very sorry I put you through this. I honestly thought it would have been dropped because we had no evidence, nothing solid anyway. I will pay your attorney's fees and your parents will get their 20 percent bond back. I noticed a couple of things while watching you. Can I talk to you in private first, and then I will have Penelope join us?"

Penelope nodded at Kris, so she stepped back with Richard. "Mrs. Parker, I can read body language pretty well, and I am first going to say, live your truth. More people are aware of what that is, even if you are not. Secondly, I saw you when the forensic anthropologist and investigator was on the stand. Your eyes lit up. Go for it. I will pay your tuition too."

"That really isn't necessary," Kris told him.

"It really is the least I can do. I am just so very sorry to have put you through it all, and I don't feel like I can ever apologize enough." He waved Penelope over and informed her of his plan with Kris's tuition. Derrick came back into the courtroom, hugged Kris, and then escorted Richard out.

Ingrid Harris was at the desk, waiting to speak to Kris. She walked over, handed Kris a card, flipped it over so Kris could see there was something on the back and said, "If you ever need anything, give me a call." As she handed the card to Kris, her index finger lightly brushed the back of Kris's hand in a very sensual way.

Kris literally felt electricity, a buzzing, move through her. She had felt it before when she was with Tess. Kris was so confused, and she did not know what to do. She was zoned out to the point that she was barely registering her family and friends around her, everyone talking at once. She finally heard her dad talking to her, telling her they were going to leave before everyone else so they could get the money back they posted for the bond. Kris nodded to let her dad know she heard him. She heard Tony tell her they were all going to dinner and as they were filing out of the courtroom, Kris caught Ingrid's eye before she left. Ingrid smiled at Kris and winked at her ever so slightly before closing her briefcase and walking out.

CHAPTER 41

When Kris met Tony, he was already in the military, and she was fairly well aware of what that life in the military realm meant. When they married, she did not really grasp the fact that there would no longer be vacations that consisted of just the two of them. Visiting back home had become a chore more than anything. Many of the visits back to St. Louis were just Kris because Tony was always too busy to take leave.

She was pretty sure it was because he did not want to leave whatever girlfriend he had at that time, so in January, when an opportunity to take a vacation presented itself, Kris booked it. She was originally going to book the trip for herself. Her favorite 80's rock star had scheduled a weeklong fan event in Port St. Lucie, Florida, and when she decided to use her Christmas money for it, she told Tony she was booking it. He decided they should go together, spend a few days in St. Augustine, and then do the fan trip, with a stop in Charleston, South Carolina on the way back.

Life had mostly returned to normal after the trial was over. Kris was working steadily at the college, fostering kittens, and was still in counseling with Adrienne. With Adrienne's help, she started a therapy group and met some amazing people through that as well. Kris was in contact with Ingrid when their schedules allowed it. Ingrid was now working for the U.S. Attorney's office in St. Louis. Even Richard would check up on Kris from time to time.

When the fan trip announcement happened, Kris was on a social media platform that set up a group page for people going. There were many people who had taken the previous year's trips and cruises and were helpful in offering advice and getting to know each other.

Kris was looking forward to meeting some of the fans, some coming from Australia, but mostly, she was looking forward to finally taking a vacation that didn't focus around going back to St. Louis and having every moment of every day there planned out for her. When she returned from those trips, she needed extra time just to decompress. She and Tony spent a few days in St. Augustine, one of her favorite places to visit. She had not been there since she was a teenager and had fallen in love with it then. She actually felt like there was some reconnection in her marriage too, although they still had not been physically intimate for quite some time. Kris had all but given up on that part of their marriage, but it still hurt, and she constantly wondered what was wrong with her. What Kris and Tony still had going for them was their strong friendship. They had fun together when they went places, even just little day trips in Virginia. The drive was just like their road trips from the start of their relationship, with lots of laughs, plus serious and not so serious discussions. They played "road trip" games and stocked up on snacks. St. Augustine was just as amazing as Kris remembered, and it was wonderful to have that experience with Tony.

They arrived at the resort in Port St. Lucie in the mid-afternoon and checked into their room for the night. Once they unpacked, they decided to go to the resort's bar and start meeting people. Only a few had arrived that day, because official check-in was not until the following day, and many of the fans would be switching rooms. They walked around the property, got some snacks from the buffet, and sat outside the bar with a cool breeze coming off the St. Augustine River. Kris introduced herself to many of the people she had talked to on social media as she recognized their faces.

Tony had gotten up to check out the golf range and a couple of other activities available, so Kris stayed where she was and talked to various people. When she was in the middle of a conversation, she heard this infectious laugh come from the bar and saw a short woman with spikey blonde hair, walking with a couple of other ladies. They were walking towards Kris, when the woman approached her, holding her hand out to introduce herself. "Hey! You are Kris, right? I am Bradie Beckett. It is so nice to finally meet you." When they shook hands, Kris felt something she had never felt before and couldn't describe. She not only felt that same electricity she had with Tess and Ingrid, but there was something more to this, and Kris could not put her finger on it.

Bradie had soft eyes and a gentle touch, and when she looked at Kris, Kris thought to herself, *I know what Richard McCullen was talking about now, and I think I am in trouble … in all the right ways.*

ACKNOWLEDGEMENTS

There are so many of my friends and family that have been a part of the process of this work, but I especially want to thank the following people for their time and input. I would not have been able to finish without you…

Tom Frase — Thank you so very much for your honesty and constructive criticism that has taken me down the long difficult road to. I am quite sure I am not the easiest person to work with (just ask my ex-husband), as I know I can become frustrated quickly at times. Know that you have made such a big difference in the way I have processed this work. Thank you for making me think about how and where I put the words to paper, and mostly, helping me evolve into the writer/storyteller I have become. Your input throughout this has been invaluable and I cannot thank you enough.

N.G. — Than you for providing me with the space and tools for being able to kick this project into gear. It is truly a magical atmosphere, and being able to relax the way I did there is the reason I was able to get so much of this done. Thank you again for sticking by me during my temporary insanity over the previous years, for your support and your "No excuses" prodding along the way. You are an amazing friend, and I am honored and blessed to have you in my life. I will push a car with you any day!

Leanne Niemczyk — I cannot begin to tell you how much I appreciate your assistance with this from the play on words with names and the brainstorming late at night in helping me create the monsters. It is beyond helpful in knowing I have a friend that can not only understand where my brain takes me sometimes but can match or better me at it. Your support and friendship is invaluable to me.

Tina D'Amico — Thank you for the input and "technical" assistance to this story, as well as the years of putting up with my B.S. Your wisdom, compassion and empathy mean more than I could ever tell you. You are fantastic at what you do (despite not doing all your homework… HA!) and I appreciate it so much.

Lindsay Trammell — I want to thank you for reading over the sections of the book that could only be clarified by you. Dr. Ward will remain a character as long as possible. You are a better teacher than you give yourself credit for, and I thank you for trusting and allowing me to be a part of your world at times.

Charissa Mayes — Thank you so much for being my legal consultant for this book. I appreciate that if you ever got tired of me asking questions (I am sure some of them the same ones), you never led on that you did. I know I personally get irritated when someone takes too many artistic liberties with either a book, a television show or movie, so I did my best to keep it "real" and kept the liberties to a minimum. Thank you for your valuable time in helping me. It is appreciated more than you can imagine.

Sheila Struckmeyer — Our meeting for the first time was not the most ideal circumstances, but I am a big believer in people being brought together for a reason. As much as the reason was a painful one, it was also such a blessing. I gained such an amazing person into my life, and I have that beautiful young man to thank as much as I do you. Love you my friend and keep FAFO going strong. Thank you so much for the photo. It is magnificent.

Liz Powell — I am sorry I lied to you in the first book. I told you that "Ronnie" would get to shoot someone in this book, but she did not. I am saving it for something much bigger in the next. I promise you will be quite happy with what Ronnie does next. Thank you again for your assistance with the finishing touches. Love you bunches woman!

ABOUT THE AUTHOR

Sharon is a native of the St. Louis area and a former police officer for the St. Louis Metropolitan Police Department. From 1997 until 2019 she lived in California and Virginia. In 2019, she moved back to St. Louis and began her second career as a Medicolegal Death Investigator for The St. Louis County Medical Examiner's Office. In addition to starting a second career, Sharon has been completing *THE WAY HOME*, and will have a contributing chapter published in a new collaborative work entitled, *Taking Back Your Power*.

Sharon published *The Ride Home*, the prequel to *The Way Home*, in 2020 and was a contributing author in *Manifesting Your Dreams: Inspiring Words of Encouragement, Strength & Perseverance*, which was released in 2019.

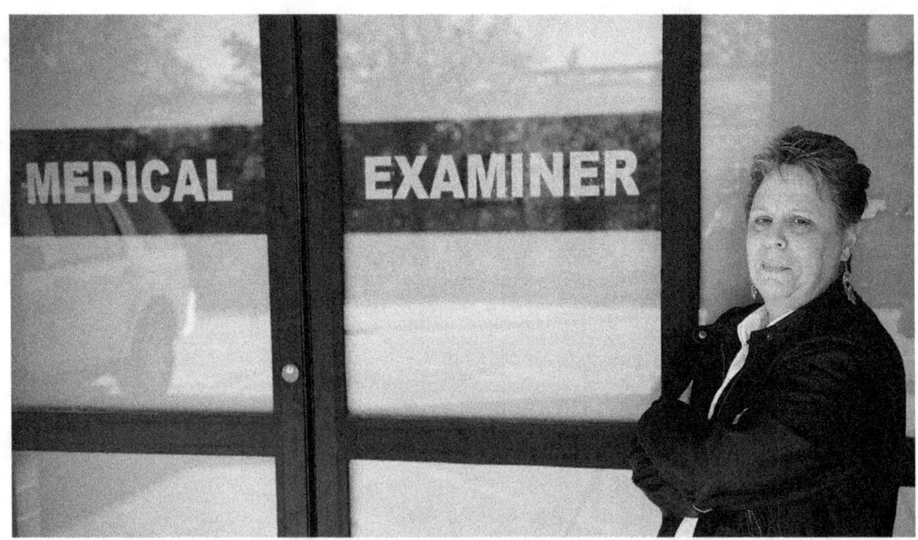